CAUGHT UNEXPECTED

. . . When he saw Clint, his eyes widened with surprise and his hand snapped upward to point his gun.

Clint's reaction was instantaneous. Coming from pure reflex, he dropped his hand down to the Colt at his side and drew the weapon before the other man could even take proper aim. Rather than take a shot, however, Clint had enough presence of mind to restrain himself. After all, killing one of the men he'd been searching for wouldn't have done him one bit of good.

With a sharp flex of his arm, Clint brought the barrel of the Colt up underneath the other man's jaw. Iron cracked against the bone, sending the running man straight to the floor. His arms and legs sprawled awkwardly as he hit the ground, making him look as if he was doing the jig . . .

THE GUNSMITH

274

GUILTY AS CHARGED

J. R. ROBERTS

JOVE BOOKS, NEW YORK

THE BERKLEY PUBLISHING GROUP
Published by the Penguin Group
Penguin Group (USA) Inc.
375 Hudson Street, New York, New York 10014, USA
Penguin Group (Canada), 10 Alcorn Avenue, Toronto, Ontario M4V 3B2, Canada
(a division of Pearson Penguin Canada Inc.)
Penguin Books, Ltd. 80 Strand, London WC2R 0RL, England
Penguin Group Ireland, 25 St. Stephen's Green, Dublin 2, Ireland (a division of Penguin Books Ltd.)
Penguin Group (Australia), 250 Camberwell Road, Camberwell, Victoria 3124, Australia
(a division of Pearson Australia Group Pty. Ltd.)
Penguin Books India Pvt. Ltd., 11 Community Centre, Panchsheel Park, New Delhi—110 017, India
Penguin Group (NZ), Cnr. Airborne and Rosedale Roads, Albany, Auckland 1310, New Zealand
(a division of Pearson New Zealand Ltd.)
Penguin Books (South Africa) (Pty.) Ltd., 24 Sturdee Avenue, Rosebank, Johannesburg 2196, South
Africa

Penguin Books Ltd., Registered Offices: 80 Strand, London WC2R 0RL, England

This is a work of fiction. Names, characters, places, and incidents either are the product of the author's
imagination or are used fictitiously, and any resemblance to actual persons, living or dead, business
establishments, events, or locales is entirely coincidental.

GUILTY AS CHARGED

A Jove Book / published by arrangement with the author

PRINTING HISTORY
Jove edition / October 2004

Copyright © 2004 by Robert J. Randisi.

ISBN: 0-515-13837-1

JOVE®
Jove is an imprint of The Berkley Publishing Group,
a division of Penguin Group (USA) Inc.
375 Hudson Street, New York, New York 10014.
JOVE is a registered trademark of Penguin Group (USA) Inc.
The "J" design is a trademark belonging to Penguin Group (USA) Inc.

PRINTED IN THE UNITED STATES OF AMERICA

10 9 8 7 6 5 4 3 2 1

ONE

Not many folks had ever heard of Waylon City, Montana. It was a big enough place, complete with a good-sized merchant district and enough distractions to keep anyone passing through occupied during their stay. A railroad line had even come through close enough for the locals to hear the steam engines as they rumbled through what had once been a peacefully quiet pass.

Unlike boomtowns that sprouted up like weeds overnight, Waylon City had deep roots that sank down almost as far back as the first settlers who picked the spot as a nice one to build a house and raise a family. The population had grown to a respectable count and most of them led pretty good lives.

The reason Waylon City went unnoticed by most everyone else in the region was simply because the locals wanted it that way. They recognized the benefit of keeping a low profile and knew the good thing they had. That sentiment could be traced all the way back to that town's first family, and there was no reason to change it anytime soon.

It only took an open set of eyes and ears for a stranger to catch on to the locals' desires to keep to themselves.

1

In fact, most travelers who passed through took a liking to the town's serenity and kept it as a quiet place to go as well. The ones who weren't so inclined were usually on their way to somewhere else and were easily distracted by the likes of distant neighbors such as Cheyenne or Deadwood.

Once arriving in places like those, it was easy to forget a quiet sanctuary like Waylon City. Either that, or the chaos in those other towns was enough to make someone want to keep Waylon City a secret that much more.

Clint Adams had been working his way to Leadville, Colorado, when he'd discovered Waylon City some time ago. He'd been following the gamblers' circuit where Leadville was always popular. During his stay in Waylon City, Clint had been almost charmed away from his original goal altogether.

The air was almost as still as it was when he was camping alone under the stars. The folks there had been easygoing and friendly once they watched him enough to know he wasn't about to stir up any trouble. They weren't stupid and they didn't have their heads buried in the sand. The folks he talked to knew who he was as well as the stories that had been tacked onto his name.

But none of that seemed to make much difference once he'd proven himself in their eyes. Clint had befriended a few locals during a card game, one of whom was the town physician, a quick-witted man everyone called Doc Cohen. It hadn't been a difficult task. All he needed to do was act civilly and appreciate the same peace and quiet that defined the town itself.

Not only did Clint appreciate that serenity; he cherished it.

It wasn't for the same reasons as everyone else who either lived there or visited Waylon City frequently. On the contrary, Clint had reasons for liking that place that only a few others could truly appreciate. Some of those others were friends of his such as Bat Masterson, Wyatt Earp, and Bill Tilghman.

Some of those were merely acquaintances like Doc Holliday or even a few others that drifted even further toward the wrong side of the law. Legal differences aside, however, Clint shared a very specific bond with all of those men, and that was a name that was recognized from one coast to the other.

Famous, infamous, or somewhere in between, every one of those men were known for something and that alone made living a normal life difficult to say the least. Granted, some men enjoyed their reputations more than others, but there were always times when a man needed to just kick back and savor the simpler things like anyone else.

For some, that couldn't happen too often because of constant requests to clean up one town or another. Others had to worry about such things as lawmen, bounty hunters, or just some angry loser at a previous card game.

Clint belonged to another group that had to worry about distractions like some loudmouthed kid who just discovered he could fire a gun and wanted to make a name for himself. Men like that were always after men like Clint the way hunters were after big game. It wasn't Clint's favorite way to think about it, but it was accurate enough.

For all of these groups, places like Waylon City were invaluable. Of course, such places also became closely guarded secrets by the folks who cherished them. If too many known men came through a place, that place became known as well.

It was that simple.

And it was for that simple reason that Clint rarely told anyone at all about Waylon City.

It had been a few years since the last time he'd spent any real time in the tranquil place. This time, he vowed it was going to be different.

When Clint headed into Montana, he'd purposely pointed Eclipse's nose toward Waylon City and was careful not to waste a moment of time that could be spent riding toward the town's limits. Like a good deal of his life, the recent month or two had been particularly hectic and Clint was anxious to slow down and let a few days slip by without risking life or limb. Perhaps Doc Cohen still lived there and was ready for another round or two of cards.

All too often, Clint had been pulled away from wherever he was going or whatever he was doing by some emergency that couldn't be left alone. Such a hectic state of affairs had happened so often that, for him, it had actually become common.

This time, he'd vowed to hurry up and get to Waylon City so he could get a room with a view of the mountains and drop out of sight for a while. His intention was to stay a week or two, but he would settle for a few days if that was all he could get before another of those distractions came along.

As soon as Clint rode into town, he could feel his muscles relaxing and his lungs filling with the cold, clean air that had blown down straight from the Rockies.

"Yes sir," Clint thought. "This stay will be a different story from the last one."

TWO

Even if he'd wanted to find something to grouse about, Clint would have been hard-pressed to come up with much of anything. From the moment he got into Waylon City, everything had been exactly as he'd hoped. Sure, the town had grown a bit since he'd been gone, but it was still the tranquil place he remembered.

There was a small stable within eyeshot of the Ridgeway Inn, which was where Clint wanted to stay. It seemed as though the town itself had been waiting for him to arrive since there was only one more stall in that stable, which suited Eclipse just fine.

Clint took his time walking down the street so he could let the quiet start soaking into his weary bones. He had his saddlebags slung over his shoulder, but he didn't even seem to feel their weight as he stepped through the front door of his hotel.

The Ridgeway Inn was a shade bigger than the stables he'd just left and had the open, comforting spaces of a cabin in the mountains. The interior smelled like aged pine and burning firewood, mingled with the first hints of roasted beef. A large desk made out of fresh mahogany took up a good portion of the lobby and was topped with a leather-bound book held open by a large red ribbon.

"Good evening," said the attractive girl behind the desk. "Welcome to Waylon City."

Clint smiled at the thin, pretty young woman. "Is it that obvious that I just rode into town? I hope I don't have too much dirt on my face or dust on my britches."

The young woman returned his smile and lowered her head slightly. She wore her shiny black hair short enough so that it bounced on either side of her face and covered her eyes like a nervous pair of hands. "Not at all. You look just fine. It's just that I know I would remember if I saw you before."

She said that last part in a tone that was slightly lower than the rest as well as with a promising upturn of her eyes. Clint may have been a little tired from the day's ride, but he wasn't blind enough to miss the signal she was sending him.

When he approached the front desk, Clint set his bags down and leaned forward on his elbows. That put his face close enough to hers that he could smell the fresh scent of her skin. She didn't so much as try to pull back.

"This place has gotten a lot better since the last time I've been through here."

Looking slightly embarrassed, she said, "Oh, so you have been here before."

"It's been years and we never crossed paths." Clint lowered his voice just a bit to match her previous tone. "I surely would have remembered that."

She smiled before stepping back so she could get a better look at the register. "We have built up some since last year. The owner's planning on putting a saloon in this summer."

"Hopefully I'll be back to see that. Do you have a room for me tonight?"

"We sure do. There's one with a view of the mountains and its own bath." She looked around as if concerned that someone was spying on her. "I'll just charge you for a regular room, though. Consider it our way of saying welcome back."

"Much obliged," he said while reaching for the pen next to the register. "My name's Clint and hopefully, I'll be taking up space around here for a little while."

The young woman gave him a wide, inviting smile. "I hope you will be, too. If you need anything at all, just ask for me. My name's Emma."

By the time he looked up after signing his name in the large book, Clint saw a key dangling from one of Emma's extended fingers. When he took the key, his own fingers brushed against some of the smoothest skin he'd felt in a while.

"All right Emma. Maybe I'll be seeing you before too long. Smells like dinner's on its way."

"It sure is. It's being served in about an hour."

"Great. I've got one hell of an appetite."

Judging by the way she looked at him, Emma was thinking that Clint may have been on the menu. Clint noticed this just before he stepped away from the desk and didn't mind it one bit.

The hotel was pretty much as he remembered, except a little more finished. It had always been big, but lots of the space had been empty or cluttered with decoration. It seemed that Waylon City had seen its fair share of prosperity since Clint had last been there. Just so long as the quiet remained, Clint didn't mind that one bit either.

Emma hadn't lied about the room. The view almost knocked Clint off his feet the moment he unlocked the door and stepped inside. Even though he'd ridden across the beautiful high country, looking at it now from that particular angle made him feel as though he was looking at a painting instead of through a large, open window.

Next to the window on one side, there was a small table with a chair. On the other side was a wardrobe and dressing mirror. A large, four-poster bed took up nearly half the room and came up higher than Clint's waist. After setting down his saddlebags, Clint sat himself down on the edge of the bed and realized it was every bit as soft as it looked. Between that and the view, Clint almost overlooked the last piece of furniture, which took up another healthy chunk of the entire room. It was a claw-foot bathtub, and stacked next to it was a pile of clean white towels as well as a bowl of salts.

Clint's eyes were still on the bathtub when he heard a knock on his door. He opened it and found Emma standing outside waiting for him.

"Would you like me to have some hot water brought up?"

"You're good. How'd you know I was thinking about taking a bath?"

"I didn't exactly. I was just thinking you looked kind of dirty."

The way she said that last word, there was no mistaking it for an insult. In fact, it made Clint think that Emma was just a little dirty herself.

And he didn't mind that one bit.

THREE

"Those old cowboys think they can just plop their fences on a bunch of land and call themselves barons! I'll tell ya one thing. It takes a hell of a lot more for someone to be considered a goddamn baron than just a fat deed and a few dozen head of cattle."

The stocky man with the face full of hair had been talking ever since dinner was served. Actually, Clint had been in the dining room of the Ridgeway Inn before dinner had been served and the stocky man had been talking even since before then.

At first, Clint had been allowing his hopes to rise every time he heard that fellow say he was just going to say "one more thing." After the last six or seven things, however, Clint abandoned all hope of the man shutting up at all. There was some light at the end of the tunnel however, since there was plenty of food being served and that at least served to muffle the other man's constant flow of bluster.

"And one more thing," the barrel-chested man said, while spitting out a couple of wet chunks of partially chewed bread. "If them so-called barons want to make some real money, they should listen to me. Hell, I gave

some advice to a man smart enough to take it ten years
ago and now he's got more money than he knows what
to do with."

Clint grimaced and tried to block out that voice, but it
boomed throughout the entire room. It didn't help that
Clint's mood wasn't the greatest to start off with. The
thought of Emma walking slowly around the bathtub in
his room was still drifting through his mind. . . .

As more hot water was brought up, the steam began to
rise, causing her white cotton shirt to cling to the front of
her body.

All the while, she stayed there and watched him with
those wide, dark brown eyes of hers, dropping little hints
about how good the bath would feel once it was ready.
She even made a playful comment about wanting to join
him in there, but merely smirked and patted Clint on the
cheek before turning on the balls of her feet and heading
for the door.

"Maybe some other time, Mister Adams," she'd said,
twitching her hips expertly and knowing full well that she
was being watched. "Right now I've got to start getting
things set up for dinner."

Clint had shaken his head and laughed slightly to himself at the fine job Emma had done in getting him so
worked up. "Now that wasn't very nice," he told her.

Stopping just outside the door, Emma turned and
looked back at him over her shoulder. "I know," she'd
said, with a crinkle of her nose that still managed to take
some of the edge off of her leaving. "But perhaps I can
make it up to you later."

And with that, she'd left him alone to have his bath.
Although the hot water felt great and washing off all that
trail dust felt even better, Clint was more inclined for a
splash of cold water after all that buildup. Having made
himself presentable and gotten into some fresh clothes,

Clint followed his nose downstairs and prepared to make everything better with a big meal.

Emma was still giving him some promising glances from across the room, which made Clint relax even more into the comfort of the inn and town in general. Of course, that peacefulness started cracking the moment he'd heard the big man spouting off from his table in the middle of the room. . . .

If he wasn't talking about politics, the oafish man was complaining about the weather. If he wasn't grousing to one of the servers bringing him his food, he was giving the entire world financial advice. Clint had been able to block it out for the first couple of minutes, but started to feel his skin twitching when he realized this constant, loud, unwanted commentary just wasn't going to stop.

Despite the fact that he'd already eaten several rolls and was just now about to start in on the steak he'd ordered, Clint felt like he'd been sitting at that table for several hours. He rolled his eyes when he heard that all-too-familiar voice boom on about yet another new topic.

"And I'll tell you one more thing," the big man snorted. "That president of ours couldn't have gotten this country into worse trouble if he just handed it over to the Mexicans!"

Up until this point, Clint hadn't wanted to look at the loud figure in the middle of the room simply because he didn't want the fellow to start talking at him. But after all this time, he couldn't resist any longer. Clint cocked his head to one side and took a look at the big man.

The general shape of the man was hard to miss, even if Clint hadn't been trying to look at him dead-on. His torso was squat and rounded, making him look like a tree stump that was well overdue to be pulled out of the ground and hauled away. His wide face was expressive and full of hair. An odd detail that Clint hadn't noticed before was that the guy's beard was surprisingly well trimmed while his mustache had been allowed to sprout nearly out of control over his upper lip.

When the loudmouth spoke, he flapped his jaw open almost as far as it would swing, exposing a cramped set of teeth that practically spilled out of him at all angles. His voice sounded like a saw grating against chipped rock. The more it could be heard, the more it grated on the ears. Judging by the looks on the faces around him, Clint wasn't the only person in the room who shared that opinion.

A boy in his teens was working Clint's section of the dining room. When he saw that kid come over to him with a fresh drink and a plate of vegetables, Clint motioned for him to come closer so he could be heard when talking to him.

"Who is that guy?" Clint asked.

Knowing who he meant without having to look where Clint was pointing, the kid rolled his eyes and answered, "That's Tony Ackerman. Do you want me to ask him to keep his voice down?"

Clint was an expert in summing up other people simply by watching their eyes and listening to the tone of their voices. It was obvious by the way the kid asked that last question that he was both anxious to ask Mister Ackerman to shut up and hesitant to put himself in the big man's sights. An odd combination, to be sure, but understandable given the circumstances.

"Would it do any good?" Clint asked.

After about half a second to think it over, the server shook his head. "Probably not. Sorry about that."

"You'll only need to apologize if you give him something else to yack about. Please tell me he's not staying in this hotel."

"No, he lives in town. He just eats here quite a bit, but once he's had his cigar, we'll be rid of him for a while.

You might want to steer clear of the Broken Axle, though."

"The Broken Axle?"

"It's the biggest saloon in town, but it's also where Mister Ackerman spends a lot of time when he's not making our customers here wish they were somewhere else."

"Ah. I see." The saloon was another new addition to the town since the last time Clint had been there.

"Hey boy," came the familiar blast of Ackerman's baritone. "If it ain't too much trouble, I'd like to get something to drink around here. That is, unless I need to talk to the manager AGAIN!"

Clint could feel the kid's hackles rising like there was a storm coming from the server's innards. "My fault," Clint said, breaking his effort to keep from being noticed. "I was having a word with him about my order."

"Well be quick about it," Ackerman shot back. "There's other people in here, you know."

After a quick thank-you, the server jogged over to Ackerman's table to see what he wanted. Clint shook his head, took a drink of his coffee, and reminded himself that not even Waylon City could be perfect all the time.

FOUR

Clint had every intention of taking the server's advice by avoiding the Broken Axle that night. His mood had taken a turn for the better once he'd had a chance to eat his steak. Of course, it helped that he was able to top it off with a complimentary piece of cake given to him by his waiter. It seemed that taking the blame for the delay in Ackerman's service helped the kid out even more than Clint had thought.

The funny thing was that when he looked around, Clint found he wasn't the only table that had been presented with cake in that room. Once Ackerman left the dining room, things immediately dropped down to the levels that Clint had remembered.

Once again, the night became quiet, and once again, his nerves started to loosen up underneath his skin.

With the meal still filling his belly, Clint stepped out of the Ridgeway Inn and pulled in a deep breath of wintry air. The cold was tightening its grip upon the air and the effects could be felt even more in the northern part of the country. Just as Clint closed his eyes and began to soak up the special kind of calm that came only in the mountains at that time of year, his ears were rattled by a very unwelcome sound.

"Y'ask me, if that damn restaurant wants to stay in business, they should use some common sense."

It was Ackerman. Glancing over toward the sound of the stout man's voice, Clint found him puffing on a cigar in the company of two others who'd been sitting at his dinner table.

"Food's just fine, I guess," Ackerman squawked. "But the prices are too damn high. Remind me to have a word with that owner about that."

Clint could hear the voices of the others around Ackerman, but since those people were talking in normal tones, he couldn't make out every last word they were saying. Turning on his heels, Clint pulled in another deep breath and pointed himself away from the loud man and his cronies.

Unfortunately, Ackerman's voice dominated the wind itself and would not be shaken off so easily.

Clint finally had to start whistling a tune to himself as he quickened his pace until there was finally enough street separating himself from Ackerman. Once he could only hear the distant grumble of the other man's constant ramblings, Clint's smile returned and he took a walk around to see how much the town had changed.

All in all, the entire place seemed to have stretched out a bit since the last time he'd been in town. Even more than the expansions he'd seen when he'd first arrived, Clint noticed that practically every street was a little longer and every storefront was just a bit more decorated. It made him smile to see the town doing so well. He didn't know how many times he'd set his sights on visiting an out-of-the-way place only to find a desolate husk when he arrived.

Especially that far west, places had a tendency to

shrivel up and blow away. Not only was Clint glad to find Waylon City still right where he'd left it, but he was happy it was prospering. The town deserved to do well. He only hoped it didn't fall into decline the way many other places had done before it.

As he thought about such things, Clint found himself rounding a corner, which brought him into the entertainment district. The sounds of pianos being played and songs being sung mingled with the frozen breeze. There weren't many people on the street where Clint was walking, but that changed a little farther up the boardwalk.

The nightlife of Waylon City was nothing when compared to such places as Tombstone or Dodge, but there was enough to keep someone occupied and that was all Clint needed for the time being. Instinctually, he found himself walking toward the most inviting saloon, but stopped when he saw the ornate sign on the front of the building.

The Broken Axle.

Those words were painted in large letters over a simple drawing of the namesake. But more than just an image of a busted wagon, the sign brought up something that nearly stopped Clint in his tracks. He caught himself before he walked into the very saloon he'd been planning to avoid. No matter how good it looked from the outside, Clint only had to imagine that Ackerman was inside and that was enough for him to pass it by.

Waylon City might not have been a gambler's heaven, but there was certainly more than one saloon in town. Clint picked out one that was just a bit farther down the street. He didn't even look at the name of the place. All that mattered to him was that Ackerman was in the Broken Axle and he was in a different place himself.

The saloon Clint wandered into was smaller and therefore not so hectic. There was even a large fireplace taking up a good portion of one wall, which reminded him of a hunting lodge. Adding to that image was a row of stuffed animals' heads mounted along the wall over the mantel.

As if he needed any more incentive to stay, Clint spotted not only a row of card tables covered in well-maintained felt, but several serving girls dressed in white skirts and blouses that were open far enough to display their ample cleavage. Once again, Clint felt happy just to be where he was, and as soon as he ordered a beer, he started looking for a spot to gamble.

"We're one short over here if you mean to play some cards," one of the men at a table said to him.

Clint pulled out the chair he'd been offered and sat down. "Don't mind if I do."

"Hope you don't mind poker."

"Mind?" Clint asked with a wry grin. "I would have insisted."

"Then you're in the right place. Polly, set us up with another round, will you?"

The waitress that had taken Clint's order brought over his beer and nodded once. "I'll be right back." When she spun around to walk back toward the bar, her skirts kicked up just enough to show the fine curves of her muscled calves. Her breasts bounced with every practiced motion, surely intended to increase her gratuity, but also increasing the smile upon Clint's face.

"And let's have another for our new friend, here," the man added, nodding toward Clint. "If he has any luck here, he can buy the next round. If not, at least he'll have a full belly if not full pockets."

Clint took the good-natured jibe as it was intended and tipped his hat when the second beer was placed next to the first. With four players now sitting at the table, the cards were dealt and the game was set into motion. The conversation around the table was friendly and the stakes were just high enough to keep things interesting.

No more than an hour had gone by before Clint's good humor was once again shattered.

"Damn place is too damn crowded!" came Ackerman's voice as he barged into the once cozy saloon. "I just hope to God the barkeep at this place has figured out which brand of whiskey to serve or else there's going to be some hell raised in here!"

As Ackerman came in, his entire group of followers came in with him. Not only that, but he seemed to have picked up a few more along the way. The stench of his cigar blew in with the wind, which no longer seemed brisk, but just plain cold.

"Barkeep!" Ackerman shouted while slamming his hand against the bar. "Set us up with some good, quality drinks and if I taste one drop of the bad stuff, I'll have your hide!"

Clint rolled his eyes and shifted back around to face the rest of his table. "Jesus Christ," he muttered.

FIVE

"So what's yer story?" Ackerman grunted as he pushed a chair up to Clint's table and plopped down into it.

Over the last couple of minutes, Ackerman and his group had been keeping surprisingly to themselves. So much so, in fact, that Clint had actually been able to get his mind focused on his game rather than whatever manure was spilling out of Ackerman's mouth.

The barrel-chested guy seemed to sense that he wasn't being watched any longer and took it upon himself to remedy the situation. His chair creaked as he leaned back and fired up two matches at once so he could engulf the tip of his cigar in flame. He'd chewed so much on the other end that it glistened with saliva next to his fat lips.

"You there," Ackerman snorted. "I know everyone here but you. Are you deaf or just too busy to answer a man's question?"

Clint fought back the urge to swat the cigar from Ackerman's face and put on a polite smile instead. "Sorry about that. I was just thinking about my game here."

"Well these here fellers won't mind waiting for a moment while you answer my question." When he said that, Ackerman looked around at the other three seated at the table. The expression on his face reflected that he couldn't think of anything better for anyone else to do than deal with him.

Two of the others shrugged and the other man sighed under his breath. They were all obviously annoyed and Ackerman obviously didn't give a damn.

Grinning proudly around his cigar, Ackerman said, "See? They don't mind, so how about you tell me what brings you here to Waylon City?"

"Just taking in the scenery," Clint said, trying to appease the other man without encouraging him. "Thought I'd play some cards before getting some sleep."

"Sleep? Huh. Sleep's for babies, sick folks, and them that don't have any gumption. Plenty of time to sleep when you're dead!"

"Yep."

"I'll tell you one thing—"

"Yeah," Clint said before he could stop himself, "I'll bet you will."

That caused Ackerman's head to snap back as though he'd been rapped on the nose. He didn't seem angry at first, but more as though he just couldn't believe what he'd heard. "Excuse me?"

Although Clint hadn't meant to provoke anything, he wasn't entirely unhappy about what he'd said. Even so, he put on an apologetic smile and shrugged. "Nothing. We're all just in the middle of a game here. There's money at stake. I'm sure you understand."

Ackerman fixed his eyes on Clint and gave the collection of coins and bills in the middle of the table a quick glance. "Money at stake, huh? You call that a pot? I call that a pile of loose change!" He then turned around to look at the others he'd brought with him and started to laugh.

The rest of his group knew the roles they were playing and started laughing right along with him even though they hadn't heard the joke. For the most part, none of those others looked to be much trouble. There were a few who Clint figured could be trouble and they were even wearing guns. But none of them had the look of hired muscle and they all surely seemed to be far from the killing sort.

"So what do you say?" Ackerman asked as he reached into his breast pocket and pulled out a wad of ten-dollar bills clipped together. "How about we make this a man's game?" With that, he dropped the entire money clip onto the table and looked around as though he'd challenged the devil himself.

Nobody at the table stirred.

Everyone else in the saloon seemed well versed in pretending not to hear Ackerman, which left Clint alone to answer the challenge that was still written all over the other man's flabby face.

"I don't know what the problem is here," Clint said, "but whatever it is, there's no need for it. All I wanted was a friendly game of cards."

Ackerman's eyes remained fixed on Clint as though he was staring at him over a gun barrel. "No problem. I'm after the same thing as you."

Clint's first reaction was to say something to antagonize Ackerman just so he could put a real face on the tension in the air. Then he realized that what he really wanted was to create a reason for him to let out the steam that had been building up inside of him thanks to the asshole chomping on his cigar.

Letting out a breath and forcing himself to cool off, Clint came up with another way to vent. "All right then. If you want to raise the stakes, I think I can accommodate you."

"All right, then," Ackerman sneered. "Let's play some poker."

SIX

The first thing to happen once Clint accepted Ackerman's challenge was for the table to lose one of its players. Seeing that the once friendly game was now going to cost him some serious money, a middle-aged shop owner who'd been the source of some good jokes over the last several hands got up and left. He said his good-byes and even tossed a polite nod toward Ackerman, but it was obvious that he was angry at being forced out.

Ackerman responded with a mocking pout and stretched out even more as if he was entitled to every inch of the newly available space. Besides him and Clint, that left a banker named George and a grizzled gray-haired man everyone called Old Man Tate.

George wore a tailored, though not fancy, pin-striped suit complete with a polished watch chain crossing his belly. He was bald except for a ring of salt-and-pepper hair that looked more like it had been drawn onto his scalp with a pencil.

Old Man Tate wore layers of clothes that looked older than the saloon he was gambling in and wore his thick, flowing gray hair like a lion wore its mane. Despite his appearance, he didn't have any trouble raising the stakes and had yet to crack a smile all night. Even Clint had to admire a poker face that solid.

"You sure any of you ladies don't want to leave?" Ackerman asked, casting his eyes toward Old Man Tate and George in turn. When he looked at Clint, he nodded and said, "Let's do this."

Of course, Ackerman grabbed the cards and insisted on dealing first. The first round of betting was more than the original players had been playing for all night, but wasn't anything too bad. Old Man Tate threw in three of his cards, Clint did the same, keeping a pair of aces, while George and Ackerman tossed in one and two cards respectively.

Old Man Tate and George both dropped out when they saw their new cards and though Clint didn't get anything else to compliment his original hand, he stayed in with his two aces.

"You sure you want to sit on that pair?" Ackerman asked smugly.

Clint smirked and nodded. "Don't expect me to be impressed because you noticed I kept two cards." With that, he threw in a two-dollar raise.

"It's your funeral."

Another round of betting brought the pot up to ten dollars. This time around, Clint wasn't as concerned with winning as he was for getting a feel for his primary competition. It wasn't half as hard a task as it normally was, mainly because Ackerman had already done much of Clint's work for him. It was the one and only time when Clint was happy the other man had such a big mouth.

Ackerman didn't even try to hide how pleased he was with himself when he nodded and tossed in another couple of dollars. "Wasn't exactly what I was after, but it'll do nicely."

"We'll see." As he said that, Clint matched the bet. "What do you have?"

"Two ladies. And they are so pretty!"

Clint almost couldn't believe how easy it had been to read the man. Ackerman seemed genuinely pleased with the cards he'd been dealt and his reaction when he showed his hand only proved it. Now it was time for another little test.

"They are pretty," Clint said. "But not as pretty as these."

When Clint's aces dropped onto the table faceup, Ackerman seemed angry at first, but got himself under control quickly. "Lucky deal, mister. That's all it was."

Even so, Clint could tell that that simple victory had gotten under Ackerman's skin. The man was either trying to run some kind of game by faking his easily read expression or was just so obnoxious that he took every single gle loss as a kick below the belt.

Old Man Tate got the deal next and he flipped out the cards while giving a pleased smirk to Clint while the pot was pulled in.

Clint got three cards to a club flush and discarded the other two when it was his turn. George only dropped one again, Ackerman chucked two, and Old Man Tate threw in his entire hand.

"Think I've been jinxed," Tate said, giving Ackerman a sideways glance.

Still gnawing on his cigar, Ackerman replied, "Then take it like a man. I don't like hearing no babies crying at a card table."

Clint didn't get a damn thing to complement his hand, but stayed in so he could watch Ackerman a bit more. Both of the other men stayed in as well and Ackerman seemed so pleased with himself that he looked about ready to bust.

After nudging the pot up a bit more, Clint dropped out. He was fairly certain George had something to work with and any fool could have seen the same written on Ackerman's smug face. After taking a moment to think, Clint shrugged and tossed in his cards.

"Too rich for ya, huh?" Ackerman asked. "Well, I don't blame you. Let's just see if Georgie here has the same good sense."

Although he didn't seem anxious to look the loud-mouth in the eyes, George bumped up the bet by another ten dollars.

Ackerman whistled and gave the banker a condescending smirk. "Oh my, what have we here? Looks like George wants to step up with the big boys. Well that's all right. I can take your money and not lose a wink of sleep. I'll see that bet and raise it another ten."

George took a moment to look over his stack of chips, which made Ackerman think he had the right to celebrate.

"Go on and drop out, Georgie. You don't have any status to live up to anyhow."

"Raise you five," George replied in a somewhat squeaky tone.

Ackerman squinted as he dramatically studied George's pile of chips. "Tell ya what, Georgie. Let's make this interesting, because I'm so bored I'm about to spit."

Clint rolled his eyes as he watched Ackerman make an absurd show of raising the bet by the exact amount of chips that were piled in front of the banker. To be even more obnoxious, the man with the cigar started to put on one more chip, which would have forced George to come up with some other way to match the bet.

SEVEN

Dangling that extra chip over the pot, Ackerman finally closed his hand around it and slammed it onto the table in front of him. "Nah! I'll let it stand at that. You probably don't even have the stones to match it anyway."

The muscles in George's jaw tensed and the color flushed into his face. Looking around nervously, he found that nearly everyone in the saloon was watching and waiting to see what he would do.

"Fine," George said, shoving all his chips forward. "If you insist."

Clint placed his hand on the banker's wrist, stopping him before his bet joined the rest of the pot. "You don't have to do this, George."

"I know. It's fine."

Clint didn't move until he was sure that the banker truly meant to go through with what he was doing. Once he knew George really wanted to go all in, Clint moved away and left him to it.

"Georgie's a big boy," Ackerman chided once his raise had been officially called. "Or at least he thinks he is. Let's see if he's big enough to beat these." With that, he laid his cards on the table. He had two pair: nines over fives.

Without making a sound or even batting an eye, George showed everyone the two pair he had: kings over sixes.

Clint couldn't keep himself from letting out a surprised laugh, which couldn't be heard over the delighted whoop that came from Old Man Tate.

"Well I'll be goddamned!" Tate shouted as he reached across the table to shake George's hand. "I sure as hell didn't see that one comin'."

"Neither did I," Clint said frankly, giving the banker a slap on the back. "Well played. It looks like we know who's buying the next round of drinks."

Ackerman had yet to say a word.

His teeth chomping down so hard on his cigar that he almost bit it in two, Ackerman had his hands resting on the edge of the table with his fingers curled down over the edge. "Well played, my ass," he snarled. "That was cheating. I had that hand. That pot is mine."

Clint could feel the rage building up inside of the other man like heat from a nearby fire. He kept his face and voice calm, however, so as not to fan the flames. "No need to worry. Just bad luck, that's all. It happens to the best of us. Polly, how about getting a drink here?"

"Fuck you and your bad luck," Ackerman said. This time, his words came out more as a growl. Shifting his eyes back to George, he added, "And you can stuff every one of them drinks up your ass. I want my money back."

Although George looked uncomfortable, he didn't stop raking in his winnings. "I played my hand and won. Keep playing and you can probably win it all b—"

"Are you deaf? I said I want my money back."

The banker swallowed uncomfortably, but kept his chin up. "No," he said.

"What?"

George cleared his throat and said, "No. I won this fairly. It's mine."

Ackerman's hand snapped forward quicker than anyone might have guessed could come from a man of his size and build. His teeth were bared and his chubby fingers reached out to take hold of George's neck as he practically threw himself over the table.

Reacting out of pure reflex, Clint managed to grab Ackerman's wrist, stopping the other man's hand only an inch or so away from George's throat. He found he had to exert a fair amount of strength to keep Ackerman at bay and even more to break the barrel-chested man's momentum.

"Don't be stupid," Clint warned.

The moment Ackerman looked away from him, George scooted away from the table and jumped to his feet, taking as much of his winnings as he could gather up in both arms.

Glaring at Clint with enough anger seething behind his eyes to practically send steam out of his ears, Ackerman said, "So now you're calling me stupid?"

Clint knew right then that there was nothing he could say to make anything better. Before he could even try, however, he felt Ackerman shift his weight and pull away from him. The other man's strength wasn't enough to break Clint's grasp, but it was enough to gain him a few more inches between them, which was all Ackerman wanted to do.

Even though he could see the punch coming, Clint wasn't in much of a position to do anything about it besides twist his upper body so he could protect his face. The blow pounded against the side of his head, sending a ringing through his ears and a few sparkling lights in his eyesight.

Clint kept hold of Ackerman's wrist, even as he got

his legs beneath him and stood up from his chair. From the corner of his eye, he could see that George and everyone else who'd been nearby had had enough sense to move back from the table. That was why he'd wanted to keep hold of Ackerman for so long, so Clint let the other man's wrist go.

"Who the hell do you think you are?" Ackerman asked, lashing out with another powerful swing.

Clint ducked under the punch and delivered a jab straight up into Ackerman's gut. He may not have been proud of it, but he couldn't deny how good it felt to feel his fist sink in as Ackerman crumpled around it.

Clint had been in plenty of scuffles, most of which were a hell of a lot worse than some fistfight in an otherwise quiet saloon. His instincts had become very honed to deal with situations like those and they were screaming at him to make sure his opponent was truly down for the count. Ackerman was still sputtering and trying to curse and as he stepped back, he put his chin perfectly in line with Clint's knee.

All it would take was a sharp upward pull of his leg and Clint could have put Ackerman down for the count. But when he looked down at the other man, Clint noticed it took all Ackerman had to stay upright, despite the fire that still raged in his eyes.

Clint pushed back his impulse to knock Ackerman completely onto his ass and stepped back. Looking around the saloon, he spotted each of the people who'd come in with Ackerman and stared them down one at a time. Despite the dirty looks he got from the cronies, Clint didn't get one reason to worry about any of them. Apparently, he'd been correct in thinking they were drinking companions and not hired muscle.

"I think I'll be going now," George said as he walked hastily to the door.

The barkeep seemed more concerned about the table

and chairs that had been knocked over than anything else. "I think both of you should go," he said more to Clint than Ackerman. "I'll need to tell Marshal Packard about this."

"Go ahead," Clint told him. "I'm staying at the Ridgeway Inn if he wants to find me." And with that, he started walking for the door himself.

"Don't turn your back on me, cocksucker!" Ackerman spat through a slight wheeze. "I still say you cheated and since that banker ran off, I mean to get my money from you!"

Clint kept walking and waved off the threat. "You're welcome to try."

He could hear the heavy footsteps coming up behind him, so Clint timed his own steps accordingly. By the time he was at the door, Clint could tell that those footsteps were about to roll right over him so he spun around and snapped his fist out in a straight, powerful jab.

The punch caught Ackerman right on the nose, dropping him to the floor.

"You can tell your marshal about that, too," Clint said and then left the saloon.

EIGHT

When Clint walked through the door of the Ridgeway Inn, he was already feeling better. Part of that was because of the night air that he'd taken in during his walk, but another part of it was because of the swollen ache in his right hand that had come from punching Ackerman in the face.

He wasn't the sort who took pleasure in hurting anyone, but when that anyone was actually someone like Tony Ackerman that was a different story. Clint Adams was only human, after all.

The moment he'd gotten away from the saloon district, Clint felt the quiet he remembered flow back into the town. His hotel was just as quiet too, until he was spotted walking through the lobby and heading for the stairs. When that happened, there came a flurry of welcomes and "good evening's" partnered with waves and friendly nods.

There also came a burst of motion as one of the slender figures watching the door from another room came rushing in to intercept him. Emma's face was aglow with a wide smile and she seemed so excited that she was about to bust.

"I heard about what happened," she said so quickly that Clint could just recognize the words.

His eyes widened slightly, but he didn't pull away when he felt Emma slip her arm around his own. "What did you hear?"

"About you and Mister Ackerman. Everyone heard."

"But I just came here straight from that saloon. How could you know about that fight already?"

Now her eyes widened and she squeezed his arm a little harder. "There was a fight? We only heard that you and Mister Ackerman were having some words and that you challenged him to a big poker game!"

"Well, I don't know if I really challenged anyb—"

"And we also heard that you were a good enough player to take that asshole for everything he's worth. That came from someone around here who recognized your name."

"I'm flattered, but—"

"So tell me about this fight." Pausing just long enough to catch her breath, Emma glanced down at Clint's hand and saw the redness and cuts on his knuckles. "Oh my God, you did get into a fight! Are you all right?"

Suddenly, the front door swung open and a man in his late forties stuck his head in to look straight at the older woman behind the front desk. "Tony Ackerman just got knocked out at Farrell's" was all he said before pulling his head from the door and closing it.

Clint looked over to Emma. When she looked at him after taking her eyes away from the front door, she grinned sheepishly and shrugged.

"Small town," she said by way of a quick explanation.

She walked with him up the stairs and to his room. When he got to his door, Clint unlocked it and stopped before going inside. Although she'd let go of him so he could work his key in the lock, her hands never completely left him and kept in contact either with his shoulder, arm, or back.

"I've got something I need to tell you," she whispered.

"What is it?"

"Not out here." Glancing up and down the hall, she added, "Not where everyone can hear."

Clint opened the door and held it open for her. Watching the shift of her hips as she stepped into his room, he waited for her to get all the way inside and turn around to face him before leaving the hallway himself. The door shut with a solid thump and without thinking about it, he locked it behind him.

Moving up close to her, Clint extended his arms slightly so his hands could brush against her hips. Emma didn't even start to move away. In fact, she shifted comfortably in his grasp, allowing him to feel the smooth curves of her hips against his palms.

"What did you need to say?" Clint asked.

Emma was a slender woman, but her trim body filled out her simple clothes just right. She gave Clint an even better sample of her figure when she pressed up against him and brushed her hair against his neck. Her hands fell on top of his, guiding them up and down slightly along her sides as she slowly shifted her hips back and forth.

"I wanted to say how sorry I was," she whispered.

Clint moved his face down a little closer until his lips brushed against the top of her ear. "Sorry for what?"

Emma drew in a short breath, trembling slightly when Clint let his tongue flick gently over her earlobe. "Sorry for making you wait this long." As she said those words, she closed one hand tightly over Clint's while letting the other hand slip down between his legs.

Her small hand found his hardening penis instantly, massaging it through his jeans until she could feel his erection becoming more and more prominent. Still rubbing her body against him as he kissed her ear and neck,

Emma started to let out small, trembling moans to let him know where she wanted to be kissed.

Ever since the first time she'd been in his room, Clint was waiting for this moment to come. He knew that she'd been waiting for it as well and now that it was here, every second of that waiting was about to pay off. Even more than that, he was glad for the wait, since the feel of her body beneath his hands wouldn't have been nearly as erotic without it.

Taking occasional peeks up from what he was doing, Clint moved Emma slowly back toward the bed. The room was a pretty good size; however, there was a bathtub in between them and the destination he had in mind. Every step of the way was another experience for Clint. Now that he had his hands on her, he could feel every shift of her weight as her tight little body writhed and twisted to conform to his own.

When she felt the back of her leg bump against the tub, Emma locked her hands around the back of Clint's neck and hopped up so she could wrap both legs securely around him. He was surprised at first, but quickly adapted to the situation by cupping her behind with both hands and carrying her the rest of the way to the bed.

Having reached the bed, Clint stopped and massaged her perfectly round bottom before lowering her onto the mattress. "Apology accepted," he said.

NINE

Clint laid Emma down on the bed and moved his hands slowly along the length of her body. Without any lit lanterns in the room, all he had was the scant light that came in through the window to give the room a slightly pale glow. Although he couldn't see much with his eyes, he could map out her every curve using his hands, which was exactly what he preferred to do anyhow.

Turning her head and chewing gently on her lower lip, Emma savored the feel of Clint's hands upon her while aching to feel more. By the time she felt him unbutton her blouse and slip his fingers beneath the soft material, she was already feeling the first tingles starting beneath her skin.

Clint was aching to tear her clothes off and let her do the same to him, but prolonging the moment was making him savor every last second. What had started out as a kind of game to see who could keep a straight face the longest was now something else. Holding themselves back even slightly had become a part of their lovemaking. Even though Clint hadn't even fully removed a single piece of clothing from her, he felt as if they'd been in each other's arms for hours.

Finally peeling open her blouse the rest of the way, Clint exposed her pert little breasts, which were topped with penny-sized nipples that were standing fully erect. He watched her face as he brushed his thumb over the little brown nubs, and she pressed her head back against the bed and moaned a little louder.

Crawling on top of her, Clint slid both hands along her bare breasts, cupping them and sliding his hands away only so he could lean down and run his tongue along first one nipple and then the other. His hands fit perfectly beneath her breasts and when he gently squeezed them, he placed a line of kisses between them leading up to her neck.

By the time his lips got to her mouth, Emma was well beyond the point of savoring the moment. Her body craved him the way a starving woman craved a healthy meal and when she looked up at him, there was a similar kind of hunger in her eyes.

Clint saw that hunger and was feeling it himself as well. He also felt her anxious hands taking hold of his shirt and pulling it open so hard that a few buttons sailed through the air and scattered upon the floor. She practically shoved him onto his back as she worked him out of his clothes. All the while, Clint's own hands were busy stripping her until they were both naked in the moonlight.

With his back still pressed against the mattress, Clint was just about to get up when he felt Emma climb on top of him. Both of them moved as their instincts told them, leading to a heated tangle of arms and legs. They would say something every now and then, but only in one or two words.

It wasn't the time to talk. It was the time to act and both of them knew exactly what they wanted from the other.

Emma kissed Clint again and again as her hands rubbed against his chest. He could feel the wetness between her legs as she rubbed against him, grinding her moist vagina against his rigid cock, but not yet wanting to let him inside.

Clint was letting his instincts take over as well. His hands roamed where they pleased, gliding over the smooth contour of her backside, along the supple line of her spine, and against the trim roundness of her breasts. Whenever his fingers drifted between her legs, Emma's breath would quicken and the fire in her eyes would flare up.

Straddling his chest, Emma reached behind her and massaged Clint's penis with one hand. She rubbed him with just the right amount of firmness without losing her soft touch. He followed her lead and traced a line down the front of her body until two fingers came to a stop over her clitoris.

"Oh god, Clint," Emma moaned, arching her back and gyrating against his hand. "That's it. Right there."

Just as her body started to tremble with an approaching orgasm, Emma took Clint's hand by the wrist and pulled it upward so she could wrap her lips around the fingers that he'd just been using on her. Just watching the way she used her mouth, combined with the way she looked at him while she did it, was enough to send a tremble through Clint's body as well.

He could feel her hips grinding against him in powerful, wanton thrusts. And even though he wasn't inside of her, Clint's blood was still racing through his veins and his erection became even harder. Emma scooted back so she could rub the slick lips of her pussy against his cock, teasing him with what they both wanted so much.

Just when he shifted to get inside of her, Clint felt Emma move once again on top of him. She was tormenting him, but it was in a way that they both enjoyed. He could tell that she was savoring the moments every bit as much as he, but there was something else in her eyes as well. It was that instinctual drive that moved her to the next place she wanted to be.

After turning herself around so her back was facing him as she straddled his chest, Emma wrapped both hands around his rigid penis and slowly moved back. Her hips shifted farther up along his chest and it didn't take more than a second for Clint to know what she was after. Once she was just a little closer, he reached out to grab her hips and pull her onto his face.

She arched her back and let out a pleasured, if somewhat surprised, moan when she felt Clint's tongue slide between her legs. Emma's breath caught in her throat and she couldn't even move for the next minute or two as Clint tasted her inner thighs and then finally slid his tongue inside. As he kissed and licked her, Clint kept his hands moving on her body. He massaged her hips at first, but then moved his hands up over her back and along her sides.

Once she was able to catch her breath again, Emma lowered her mouth down to see what she could do to Clint to drive him as crazy as he was driving her. Judging by the noises he made and the motion of his body, she was doing a damn fine job on her own.

Clint was so wrapped up in what he was doing that he almost forgot about what she might do in return. Emma's body tasted sweet and she responded to every flick of his tongue in a way that made him want to taste her for hours on end. When he felt her lips wrap around his cock, it felt so good that his heart skipped a beat.

Her tongue slid down his length while her lips pressed in tightly around him. She didn't hesitate to take every inch of him into her mouth and in fact seemed to devour him hungrily. Soon, her head was bobbing up and down between his legs so quickly that Clint thought the room was spinning.

Again listening to the impulses of her body, Emma

suddenly sat up and let out one more moan as Clint's tongue made another circle around her clitoris. After that, she moved down so she could straddle his hips and position his cock between her legs.

Her vagina was dripping wet and she couldn't wait one more second before taking him inside of her. Once she felt the tip of his penis between her lips, she lowered herself down and was suddenly stopped by two strong hands on her hips.

"What?" she asked breathlessly, turning around to find Clint smiling up at her.

Cupping her firm behind in both hands, Clint was enjoying the feel of her while also preventing her from moving. "You think you get to call all the shots around here?" he asked, knowing that every moment he made her wait was pure torture.

"Please," she purred. "I want it so bad."

Hearing that, Clint let her down just low enough for the end of his penis to enter her. At that moment, he felt her entire body tense and she let out a gasp when he pulled out again. Her entire body was trembling in his hands so much that Clint could practically feel the orgasm that was only moments away from exploding within her.

He pushed his hips up slightly, entered her, and left it inside for a moment. Emma let out another gasp and grabbed both of Clint's legs. She wasn't struggling against him, but was now letting herself be directed and enjoying every moment of the ride.

From where he was laying, Clint had one hell of a view. Emma's slender figure was on display in the moonlight and looked every bit as good from behind as it did from the front. The curve of her spine was a delicate line that traveled all the way down to the splendid form of her tight buttocks.

Finally, Clint lowered her down and allowed himself to slide all the way inside of her. The relief that brought

could be felt in both of their bodies and became something
more when he started pumping vigorously in and out of
her.

Before long, she was moving along with him and
Clint's hands were busy elsewhere on her body. They
spent the next several hours both giving in to and prolonging their desires, making the night something truly
for them both to remember.

Clint had come to Waylon City because of the place's
peace and quiet. There would be time enough to enjoy
that when they were both spent and lying silently in the
darkness.

TEN

The next morning, Clint slept in until well past dawn. For a man used to rising with the sun to get a good start on the day's ride, that was an awfully long time to sleep. His eyes opened on their own just before the first rays of the sun could be seen and again after they'd made their appearance. Both times, however, he closed them again so he could enjoy the warm comfort of Emma sleeping beside him.

When he could no longer remain laying down, Clint got up and climbed into his clothes. The smell of breakfast was heavy in the air and his stomach immediately began to grumble when he caught the scent of ham and eggs being fried.

"Care to join me?" Clint asked after watching Emma slide into her own clothing.

She shrugged and shook her head. "I'd love to, but I might get in some trouble if I showed up to eat breakfast instead of serve it. I'm already about three minutes away from being late as it is."

Clint looked at the small clock on the table next to the bed and checked it against his own pocket watch. It wasn't as late as he'd thought it was at first. Still, he was

41

so rested that he felt as though he'd slept through an entire day and into the next.

"Take your time," Emma said, running her hand over Clint's face as she walked toward the door. "I'll see you downstairs."

Clint wasn't in much of a hurry, but his instincts quickened his steps all the same. The rumbling in his belly was turning into a roar and once he stepped out into the hall where the smell of the food was stronger, it was all he could do to keep from running down to the dining room.

Unlike most other small towns, Waylon City seemed to have gotten on with its life as usual in the wake of the big happening from the night before. Clint got no more than his fair share of nods and glances, most of which were only of the polite variety. Folks around him weren't gossiping about any barroom brawls, and Ackerman's name didn't come up once.

All of this made Clint even happier to be in Waylon City. In fact, it made him want to stay even longer.

The entire rest of the day went by much like breakfast. It was business as usual and Clint was allowed to wander where he pleased without being reminded of any unpleasantness from the night before. He took Eclipse out for a ride to stretch the Darley Arabian's legs as well as to soak up some of the local scenery.

Even though he felt almost as comfortable in the saddle as he did upon his own two feet, Clint rarely got the chance to just sit back and ride for no other reason than to enjoy it. As much as he loved to put Eclipse through his paces, it seemed that the stallion enjoyed the run almost more than Clint himself.

The powerful horse jumped at the chance to break into a full run, streaking toward the mountains as if he meant to charge straight over them. Before he knew it, Clint was watching the sunlight fade into the west and the air become cold with the approaching night. His stomach was growling again, and with good reason. An entire day had gone by and he hadn't eaten much of anything since breakfast.

Rather than head back to the same dining room, Clint moseyed through town after putting Eclipse back into the stables for the night. He found a good place to eat before too long and ordered himself a thick steak with a baked potato on the side.

His food was served to him by an elderly woman who also turned out to be the cook, and she set the plate down while giving him a friendly smile. Clint thanked her and dug into the food, which wasn't the best he'd ever had but was good enough to put a smile upon his own face.

Despite the fact that he had every right to feel bushed after the day he'd had, Clint actually felt more energy flow into him as he made his way back to the Ridgeway Inn. Emma spotted him as he stepped into the hotel and walked over to greet him.

"I haven't seen you since breakfast," she said. "I was beginning to wonder if you just pulled out of town altogether."

"Nah. I just had a ride that wound up stretching into an event."

"It looks like it did you some good. You've got some color in your cheeks."

When she touched his face, it was innocent enough. The thoughts that were running through both of their minds, however, certainly were not.

"How much longer did you have to work today?" he asked.

"I was done since the dinner dishes were cleared away. Why?"

"Well, I thought I could take you out tonight."

"For dessert?" she asked with a hopeful, somewhat naughty tone in her voice.

"And a drink. How's that sound?"

Emma's eyes lit up and she squeezed both of Clint's hands. "That sounds wonderful! My clothes feel filthy, though. Mind if I change first?"

"Not at all. Mind if I watch?"

Despite all that had happened the night before, Emma's cheeks still flushed when she heard him say that. "If I do that, I have a feeling we won't want to go anywhere else."

"Good point."

"Why don't I meet you somewhere?" After a moment, her eyes widened again and she excitedly asked, "How about we watch a show and maybe you could even teach me to play poker?"

"Fine by me. Just tell me where to meet you and I'll be there."

"It's the best saloon in town and it's a ways off from Farrell's." Pausing, she shrugged and added, "I thought you might not want to go back there because of what happened before. Oh, not that I think you're scared or anything. It's just that—"

Clint stopped her by placing a quick kiss upon her lips. "Just tell me where to meet you," he said with a reassuring smirk, "and I'll be there."

"It's the Broken Axle Saloon on Lafayette Street. You can't miss it."

Clint's first instinct was to suggest another place. Then again, after the way things had turned out the last time he'd tried to avoid running into Ackerman, Clint figured it didn't matter where he went. Besides, he figured that shoe had already dropped.

"Sounds great," Clint said. "I'll meet you there."

ELEVEN

The first thing Clint realized when he walked into the Broken Axle was that the place had earned its reputation as the best saloon in town. In fact, it was a damn fine saloon by any town's standards and the crowd inside the place could attest to that fact.

Considering the size of Waylon City, Clint had to assume that although there were plenty of locals inside the Broken Axle, plenty others were there from out of town as well. The saloon rented out rooms upstairs and Clint had no trouble believing that plenty of travelers had come to town strictly for the Broken Axle and probably didn't leave the saloon until they were ready to leave town.

Of course, the crowd there wasn't up to Dodge City standards, but it was impressive enough. Clint stood in the doorway so he could drink in the sights and sounds that assaulted his senses from just about every angle. The bar was on the wall farthest from the door and took up one entire corner of the room. Opposite the bar was a long stage filled at the moment with a trio of garishly dressed men juggling objects in the air and tossing them between each other. The rest of the space was taken up with round card tables as well as a pair of roulette wheels.

45

All in all, Clint had to admit the place was a surprise to him. He never would have figured the Broken Axle to be so big. His mind was also put to rest by that very same fact. After all, there was plenty of space to get lost in a saloon that size and running into one man wasn't such a big concern.

The music accompanying the jugglers on stage was a rollicking number that charged up the air as well as most everyone in the room. Even Clint felt his blood pumping with the rises and falls of the sounds and a smile was firmly in place by the time he made it to the bar.

"I'll have a beer," Clint said to the barkeep who wandered over to greet him before too long. He had to repeat the order two more times before it was heard over all the ruckus, but the younger man returned quickly to make up for it.

The brew was cold and had a rich flavor to it that quickly grew on Clint after only two sips. He leaned back against the bar and watched the show until he spotted a familiar figure emerge from the crowd to walk straight toward him.

Clint's smile remained in place, but immediately lost the joy that had put it there when he got a look at the sullen, moping face that moved quickly up to a distance that was meant to be intimidating.

" 'Evening, Tony," Clint said with a polite nod. "Out for another night of cards?"

As much as Ackerman sneered and no matter how much fire was in his eyes, it couldn't overpower the dark bruises on his face that had been put there the night before. Those marks were fresh and smeared over all the parts of his face that weren't already covered with whiskers. Still, Ackerman wasn't about to give Clint an inch.

"I'll play you anywhere and any time, boy," Ackerman said. "Last night was a fluke."

Clint rubbed his chin and asked, "Are you talking

about you losing your money to George or me knocking you on your ass?"

The squat man's face twitched and he shifted on his feet like a racehorse aching to run. "Both."

"Well, I guess actions speak louder than words."

Clint said that as a way to see just how tightly wound Ackerman was. If he was going to throw a punch, it might as well come sooner rather than later. At least that way Clint would still be able to salvage a night out with Emma.

"They sure do," Ackerman said. "So why don't you be a man and let me get back some of the money I lost by taking it out of your pockets?"

"Is that a challenge?"

"You're damn right it is. I got my own table here and we can play for as long as it takes for me to clean you out. My guess is it won't take that long at all."

Clint took a look around. This time, instead of looking at the entire layout of the saloon, he was looking for anyone who seemed especially interested in his exchange with Ackerman. Even though he still had his doubts on just how dangerous the blowhard was, Clint wasn't about to stake his life on the guess that there wasn't anyone lurking nearby, waiting to back Ackerman up.

As far as he could tell, there were several faces turned his way, but nothing that wasn't to be expected when voices were raised. Most folks liked to watch a good fight, and with someone like Ackerman, Clint had no doubt there would be that many more who'd love to see the man's clock get cleaned.

"So what'll it be?" Ackerman asked, stepping into Clint's field of vision like a child craving attention. "You gonna take me up on my offer or are you gonna take in the show?"

"Actually, I just came here for the show," Clint replied.

"Next time I feel like playing cards, though, you'll be the first one to know."

And with that, Clint turned around and started walking for the door. Emma would be arriving at any time and she was definitely more interesting company than Ackerman. On a more personal note, Clint knew damn well that what he'd done had truly pissed Ackerman off and there was more than a little pleasure to be taken from that.

Clint felt a hand slap down roughly upon his shoulder.

"I ain't through with you yet, mister," Ackerman huffed. "Nobody turns away from me."

Spinning around, Clint smacked away Ackerman's pudgy hand and glared down at the shorter man. "You got some problem with me? You take it up with someone who gives a damn. I didn't do a damn thing to you except what you asked for. If you're still sore from that bruised face of yours, consider yourself lucky. Most men aren't as patient as I am."

Ackerman took a step back, feeling the heat in Clint's stare and not wanting another dose just yet. His mouth trembled as though he was going to say something, but no sound came out.

Keeping his eyes firmly locked upon the other man, Clint asked, "What is it, Ackerman? Something else you wanted to say?"

Still nothing from Ackerman.

"Good. Keep it that way and we'll both be much happier."

After taking a few backwards steps, Clint slowly turned around until he was once again facing the door. Every movement was carefully planned as a way to keep the situation from getting any worse. Things like this were never as simple as they looked. They were times when men became more like animals snarling over their territory.

Clint walked out of there in a way intended to keep

them both from losing face. He left of his own accord, defying Ackerman's challenge while Ackerman himself was simply left behind to spout off as much as he wanted once Clint was gone.

It should have been perfect.

There was no debt to be solved or old rivalry that needed to be cleared up. Hell, it seemed as if Ackerman still didn't even know Clint's name. It was just a simple case of two bulls locking horns, but more importantly, it was over.

TWELVE

At least, it should have been over.

As Clint walked out of the Broken Axle, he was already trying to picture what Emma might be wearing when she met up with him. Since the last night he'd spent with her, he'd committed every curve and every inch of her body to memory. In fact, if he thought about it enough, he could still feel her hips switching back and forth in his hands.

The night was cold and getting colder by the second. Clint felt the chill shred a path through him as a strong wind blew down the street like a stampede from Mother Nature herself. Since he was supposed to meet Emma at the Broken Axle, he made sure not to wander too far away from the place. He walked just far enough to put some distance between himself and Ackerman without getting so far that Emma might walk by unnoticed.

The street was empty. It was late enough at night that most anyone who wanted to drink or gamble was already at a saloon while everyone else was already warm by their own fireplaces. Clint picked a spot at the edge of the building and leaned against the saloon's wall so he could wait for Emma. He could feel the cold, but before too long his body got used to it.

Looking up at the stars, he stamped his feet and rubbed his hands together to get his blood flowing in the right places. He didn't know why, but the nighttime sky always seemed clearer when it was cold outside. Overhead, the stars winked down at him like shards of glass that had been thrown up in the air and frozen in place by the chilling winds.

A noise caught his ear and when Clint glanced over to see what it was, he felt his blood start to grow hotter.

"What now, Ackerman?" Clint asked. "Are you going to tell me to pick somewhere else to stand?"

The squat man's steps thumped oafishly upon the boards as he left the saloon. He slammed the door behind him as if it was some kind of show of force that was meant to impress all onlookers. The funny thing was that there was nobody else looking on.

It was just Clint and Ackerman standing out in the cold.

Just two men whose breath rose up from their faces like steam from engines that were about to collide.

"I've had enough of your lip, boy," Ackerman said.

There was something different about the man that Clint picked up on right away. His voice was trembling with failing restraint and his hand hung a little too close to the holster at his waist.

"Look, there's nobody out here watching you," Clint said calmly. "Frankly, I don't even care what your problem is anymore. Just take it somewhere else and there doesn't need to be a problem anymore."

"Too late for that."

Clint recognized the tone in Ackerman's voice. It was along the same lines as the look a man gets in his eyes when he's already committed himself to a certain path that almost inevitably led to blood being spilled. It was a shift that turned a man colder than the wintry breeze ripping through Waylon City at that very moment.

Turning so he faced Ackerman full-on, but keeping his hands hanging loosely at his sides, Clint prepared for the worst without doing anything to set it off. "Are you sure you want to push this?"

Ackerman shifted on his feet and spoke through a tightly clenched jaw. "You made me look the fool too many times."

"That was all your own doing, Ackerman. I couldn't exactly let you roll over me the way you wanted. Come on, you know that."

For a moment, there was a glimmer of reason sparking behind the anger in Ackerman's eyes. Unfortunately, it was only there for a moment and was gone the next.

"I'm gonna hurt you, boy," Ackerman said. When he spoke those words, not only was there hate in his eyes, but a hint of pleasure as well when he thought about following through on what he'd just said. "You don't come into a man's home and make him look the fool. Now you're gonna learn that lesson in a way you won't ever forget."

Clint could read the man in front of him well enough to know that Ackerman had every intention of drawing that gun of his. He'd also seen enough to know that Ackerman was anything but a real threat to him. Of course, Clint wasn't about to stake his life on that. If push came to shove, there would be no question about defending himself.

"What do you want here?" Clint asked. "You don't strike me as the killing sort."

"Maybe I am and maybe I'm not. I aim to find out."

"Don't push this any further than it has to go, Ackerman. I'm warning you."

"Oh, you're warning me? Take that warning and shove it up yer ass."

No matter how much Clint would have loved to be rid of Ackerman, he still wanted to avoid bloodshed. "I've got things to do," he said to the shorter man. "And throwing down with you isn't one of them. Go have a drink and think this over."

"You take one step and I swear I'll burn you down."

"Fine. Have it your way." Clint picked several dozen places he could put a bullet that would end the fight without killing Ackerman.

Judging by the look in his eyes, however, Ackerman had his sights set on a much more lethal target.

Ackerman's eyes narrowed and he pulled in a quick, anticipatory breath. He might as well have taken out an advertisement that he meant to draw, because that was how clear the signal was that he sent to Clint. His pudgy hand dropped down, wrapped around his pistol's grip and one finger fumbled through the trigger guard.

Clint had all the time in the world to defend himself. He found he had so much time, in fact, that he even gave Ackerman a few more seconds to change his mind. He knew that wasn't going to happen, however, and quickly saw that he was right.

Ackerman was able to clear leather and even tightened his finger around his trigger when a single shot cracked through the air. Clint's draw had been so quick that Ackerman hadn't even seen it. The bullet tore through Ackerman's leg, dropping him to the boardwalk as the cold air blew around him to make the pain of his wound even worse.

So much for the tranquility of Waylon City.

THIRTEEN

After a couple seconds had passed, Clint lowered his Colt. The smell of burnt gunpowder hung in the air. It was a foul reminder that he'd been pushed into the very position he'd been trying to avoid.

Ackerman was down on one knee, still struggling to lift his hand to take a shot. Clint wanted to warn him not to do anything so stupid. He wanted to yell at the wounded man not to push his luck any further, but Clint knew that Ackerman wouldn't have listened anyway.

But none of that mattered just then. Right when it seemed Ackerman was going to catch a second wind, he let it rush out of his lungs and fell forward onto the boardwalk. His hand relaxed around his gun and merely rested over the weapon as his eyelids drooped shut.

Clint was walking forward to take the gun away from Ackerman when he heard someone rushing toward him from the other side of the street. The steps were light, quick, and soon followed by a worried voice.

"Clint, what happened?"

Recognizing the voice, Clint turned to look over his shoulder. "Stay back there, Emma. We just had a bit of a disagreement here, that's all."

There were sounds coming from inside the saloon as well. Although the noise from there had dropped off a bit, that was only because several people inside were more than likely trying to make sure they'd heard gunshots. Footsteps approached the door and Clint knew folks would be peeking outside at any minute.

"Is . . . this the bitch . . . you've been humping while you're here?" Despite the fact that it was a painful effort to get the words out, Ackerman spat them at Clint anyway.

Emma was still running toward them both, unaware that the fight she'd heard was actually still going on.

"Just shut your mouth and sit still," Clint said, still approaching to get his hands on the other man's weapon.

"This town . . . don't need another . . . whore . . . anyhow."

And with that, Ackerman sucked in a breath, propped himself up, and lifted his gun to aim in Clint's direction.

Clint lifted his Colt and took aim as Ackerman pulled his trigger. The Colt went off first, sending a round through the air that drilled a hole through Ackerman's skull. But the man on the ground had already set his sights and committed himself to the shot.

There was no stopping him.

What Ackerman couldn't do purposely was taken care of by the last twitch that came with death. His muscles convulsed beneath his skin one last time, dropping the hammer of his pistol and spitting one round toward his intended target.

The bullet should have missed her.

It was a fluke of a shot taken in the erratic flinch of a dead man, which should have been enough factors to send that round into empty air. The only problem was that there wasn't much empty air in front of Ackerman when he died.

Clint was standing there and the rest of the dead man's

field of vision was taken up by Emma's frantically racing
form. She didn't know where she was going or what she
was getting into and if she would have known, one must
assume that she would have known to duck.

She didn't duck, however. And for that reason, the bullet caught her in her torso, low and slightly right of center.
The impact stopped her right in her tracks as quickly as
if she'd slammed into a brick wall. Her face lost all its
color and she took on an expression of stark surprise.

"Clint?" she asked, perplexed by the roar in her ears
and the sudden pain in her body. "Clint, what . . . happened?"

Clint didn't get a chance to answer her question. He
barely got a chance to twist around and catch her as she
toppled over and passed into unconsciousness. Emma's
body felt disturbingly heavy, especially when he thought
back to how light she'd been when he'd picked her up to
carry her to bed.

There was no motion in Emma whatsoever when Clint
scooped her into his arms and lowered her gently to the
ground. Her limbs dangled and swung like wet branches
and her head lolled back like a doll's. When he set her
down, Clint spotted his Colt laying in the dirt and realized
he didn't even remember dropping it.

Just then, having the pistol so close to her seemed like
an insult and he picked it up so he could holster it just to
get the weapon out of sight. Ackerman was laying nearby,
his eyes still open, but glassy and totally devoid of life.

"Emma?" Clint said, holding her face in both hands
while gently patting her cheek. "Emma, wake up, honey.
You need to open your eyes or let me know you can hear
me."

Even her head seemed heavy in his hands. When he
tried to hold her hand, Clint found that her arms felt like
thick slabs of meat. It seemed as though death itself was

sitting on her body, holding her down greedily so nobody else could claim her.

Clint pulled his hat off so he could lean down and place his ear next to her mouth. But even as he tried to listen for her breath or any sign of life, he knew he probably wasn't going to hear it. The blood was pounding through his head and the echo of the gunshots still echoed through his ears. But he listened anyhow, hoping that some other noise would make it through the rest.

With his head turned to one side, Clint caught sight of someone else looking on from a distance. After spotting that first set of eyes, he spotted another and yet another, watching the entire gruesome scene from a distance.

"You there!" Clint shouted. "Is there a doctor nearby?"

But none of those watchers moved a muscle.

"Come out of there and help us, dammit!"

Finally, all three of them shifted in the shadows, took a few steps away from where they'd been hiding, and bolted in separate directions as though their lives were hanging in the balance.

"What's going on here?" came a man's voice from the vicinity of the saloon. "I heard shooting."

Clint's hopes jumped, but before he could ask for help, he saw the man by the saloon look at him with fear as well as a measure of sheer terror.

"Oh my lord!" the man shouted while pointing toward Clint. "That man murdered Tony Ackerman and Emma Farraday!"

FOURTEEN

What the people said as they came from the saloon barely even registered in Clint's mind. He was just happy to see others coming toward them, looking almost as alarmed as he felt.

"Quick," Clint said to the first person who'd done the shouting. "She's bleeding. She needs to get to a doctor."

Two men and a woman rushed forward, nearly pushing Clint over as they ran to Emma's side. Clint didn't mind the rough treatment. In fact, he was comforted by that since it showed that they were taking the situation as seriously as it needed to be taken. He only noticed the people stooping down over Ackerman's body when they got up again and had a hasty conference with the ones looking over Emma.

As the crowd around the two bodies grew, Clint got pushed farther and farther away from Emma. He kept his eyes glued to her, however, waiting for the first opportunity that he could jump in and be of some help. Soon, the number of people huddling around Emma nearly doubled. Clint looked over to Ackerman and found only one person looking the squat body over. After another moment of that, the person reached down and closed Ackerman's eyes for the last time.

Just then, the man who'd been looking over Emma stood up and motioned at the people standing nearby. "Someone help me carry her," he said. "I need able-bodied men to take her arms and some more to take her legs."

Clint shoved himself forward, shouting as he went. "I'll help carry her. Just tell me where she needs to go."

The other man was well-dressed and wore thick round spectacles. The eyes behind the glasses narrowed as though he'd just smelled something spoiled and rotten. "Someone take that man's gun and get him under lock and key where he belongs."

"But I want to help!" Clint insisted.

"You've done enough already."

And just as Clint felt the impact of those words, he also felt several pairs of strong hands tighten around his arms. Another set of hands reached for the Colt in his holster. Clint had the strength and more than enough speed to resist his restrainers and keep his gun from being taken away. He didn't want to add more fuel to that fire, however, so he let his gun be taken and allowed himself to be dragged away from the scene.

Although he couldn't quite see what was being done to Emma or even if she was alive or dead, Clint could see plenty of concerned people fussing over her. She appeared to be in good hands and for the moment, that was the most important thing.

"Is she alive?" Clint asked, struggling to get another look at Emma as another wave of panic flowed through him. "Just tell me if she's alive or dead!"

Both of the men that had hold of Clint's arms were bulky, solid guys. They had arms like tree trunks and the solid grips of men who'd worked with their hands for most of their lives.

"What the hell do you care?" the man on Clint's right grunted.

"Probably just wants to make sure he finished her off," the second one replied. "Murdering bastard."

Clint didn't pay attention to one word of that. Once he knew that neither of those two were going to tell him what he needed to know, he focused all his attention on Emma and the locals carrying her away. His feet moved on their own accord, struggling against the other two men at first before finally falling into step with them.

"Why'd you do it?" the second man asked. "What the hell did that poor girl ever do to you?"

Clint didn't respond. His eyes were fixed on the scene that was drifting farther away by the second. He started to struggle against the men holding his arms, but quickly felt their fingers cinch around his elbows like nooses.

When people looked back at him, they did so as if they were staring at Clint through iron bars. Their eyes were filled with fear and loathing.

Emma was gone, carried away either to a doctor's office or an undertaker's parlor. Clint didn't know which.

As more and more locals were told what happened, more and more of them lent their voices to a chant that grew like a raging fire until it rang through Clint's ears.

"Hang him! Hang him! Hang him!"

FIFTEEN

After being dragged away from the scene of the shooting and taken around a corner, Clint lost some of the will to fight against his captors. The damage had been done. The worst outcome was the one that had come to pass and there wasn't anyone around who wanted a bit of help so long as it came from him.

Clint's feet carried him along between the two burly men without protest. His arms dangled within their grasp, which was so strong that he might not have been able to get them away even if he'd wanted to. As he walked, Clint pulled in a series of deep breaths meant to calm himself while his brain chewed on whatever random facts came his way.

Both of the men holding his arms smelled like smoke and iron. Their skin was smudged with a black sooty substance. That meant they were more than likely blacksmiths. No wonder they each had the strength of an ox.

"Do I get to know where I'm going?" Clint asked. "Or is it supposed to be a surprise?"

"You're damn lucky you're not being strung up," the man on his left said. "That's what we do to killers around here."

61

"Yeah," the one on his right chimed in. "We like our city nice and quiet."

Clint smirked as he hung his head between the two smiths. "I know you do. That's what brought me here to begin with. So are you going to answer my question?"

"Just shut your mouth."

Clint couldn't remember there being a jailhouse in Waylon City. Then again, he didn't exactly put those kind of places at the top of his list of places to visit while there. Jailhouses, doctors, and lawmen were the sorts of things a man only went to when he absolutely had to.

"I didn't shoot her," Clint said.

"I said shut yer lyin' hole!"

"Shouldn't you be certain of something like that before you throw anyone in a cell?"

"That ain't our concern," the one on Clint's left replied. "Say whatever you got to say to Marshal Packard."

Clint could feel the second smith's massive arms and wide shoulders shake as he let out a snuffing laugh. "Yeah. Say your piece and then you can hang."

Once he heard that, Clint figured it wasn't worth the effort to say much else to the two men dragging him down the street.

Waylon City wasn't exactly the type of place that felt it necessary to build a large jailhouse. In fact, there was no separate jailhouse at all. Instead, there were merely a few cells tacked onto the building that served as the marshal's office.

Clint was thrown into the first of those cells with almost enough force to knock him through the back wall. The smith then slammed the door shut and stepped aside so a smallish man with a scraggly mustache could fit a key into the door's lock and turn it with a well-oiled clank.

By the time Clint peeled his face off the wall and shook

the cobwebs from his head, the marshal's footsteps were already moving away from the cell. Clint stepped up to the bars to try and catch the lawman's attention, but didn't realize that one of the smiths was still standing nearby.

The hulking man's fist was wrapped around a chipped club, which he used to slam against the bars less than an inch away from Clint's hand. It was plain to see that the bigger man had missed Clint's fingers out of bad aim rather than any desire to keep from doing any damage. When he pulled back the club, it was sporting a fresh, deep dent.

"Keep quiet in there if you know what's good for you," the marshal said. "I don't have any qualms with hanging a killer with a split head and broken fingers."

After that, the marshal turned his back on the cells and sat down behind his desk. A newspaper was spread out in front of him, so he looked to that and started reading. His finger moved along the paper to mark his space and his lips moved slightly as he studied each and every word.

Clint was a man who believed in law and order. The system wasn't perfect, but it worked more often than not and without it there would be nothing but anarchy. He was a man who believed in doing things the right way even if that meant going through some inconvenient processes.

Even with all of that in mind, however, he was suddenly beginning to wish that he'd just fought his way from custody when he had the chance.

SIXTEEN

Surprisingly enough, Clint actually got some sleep that night. The cell was a far cry from comfortable, furnished with nothing more than a cot that could barely hold his weight and the proverbial pot to piss in. Having seen the inside of more than a few jailhouses, Clint was thankful that the pot in his cell had at least been emptied out since the last time it had been used.

Since the cell itself had no window, Clint only knew that morning had come because of the sunlight that streamed into the front part of the office. Getting to his feet, Clint stretched his back and rolled his head a few times to work the kinks out of his neck. He didn't think he'd be able to drift off for any length of time at all, but the arrival of dawn told him otherwise.

"Hey Marshal," Clint shouted. "Do I get any breakfast in here?"

When he got no reply, Clint stepped to the front of the cell and pressed his face against the bars to get a better look at the office. There wasn't a person in sight. Then again, there was also a good chunk of the office that he couldn't see from where he was.

"Marshal?"

Suddenly, there was the sound of something hitting the ground. It slapped against the floorboards in a way that told Clint it had to have been a book or a stack of papers. Following that was the thump of boots coming down as someone stepped into Clint's line of sight.

The face that turned his way was annoyed and at least half Clint's age. "Shut the hell up," the young man said. "Or I'll tell Marshall Packard that you're actin' up."

"Will I be getting anything to eat?" Clint asked.

"You want to eat? Hell, I would'a thought you'd be more worried about them gallows they're building outside."

"Gallows? What gallows?"

"The one we're gonna use to string you up for shootin' them two in front of the Broken Axle last night. Ain't you got no memory?"

"My memory's fine," Clint replied. "One thing I sure as hell don't remember is my trial. Shouldn't I have one of those before getting hung?"

The younger kid was leaning over to look toward the cells and seemed hesitant to come any farther. The look on his face, however, was one of arrogant bravery, which was typical for a man his age. "Ain't that just like some piece of shit killer? You cry for a trial so you can live a bit longer. Maybe you should'a thought of that before you shot them two last night."

Clint had plenty more to say on the subject, but he wasn't sure if it was worth saying it to whoever was in the office at the moment. "Where's the marshal?"

"Sleepin'."

"When will he be here?"

"I don't have to talk to you, anyhow. Just shut up."

Clint's grip tightened around his bars and he took a deep breath to steady his nerves. While it was perfectly normal for the law to be suspicious or even want to put you up for the night after a shooting, being hung after waking up was anything but. Still, he decided to wait to talk to the marshal before jumping to any conclusions.

Things couldn't have been as bad as they seemed.

With neither man making any noise, the office and cells became very quiet. It was so quiet, in fact, that Clint could clearly hear the sounds of hammers pounding nails into place not too far beyond the cell's outer wall. He told himself to keep his calm and just try to relax.

"Pull on that noose good and hard," came a voice from where the hammering had come from. "We got to be sure it won't break."

That did it.

Clint was through trying to act calm. He was through trying to go through the motions set forth by the town's law, and he was through trying to be a cooperative prisoner just to make the marshal's job easier. As far as he could tell, the marshal wasn't even going to do his job and was content to let a hangman do it for him.

Suddenly, the sounds of hammering got louder throughout the entire office. It was at that moment that Clint could hear the unmistakable sound of a trapdoor being released so it could swing back and forth upon its hinges. It was a distinctive sound that stuck in the mind of any man who'd ever been present at a hanging.

Clint could hear it especially well at that particular moment because someone had just opened the office's front door and stepped inside. Even when the door was closed again, the persistent hammering could still be heard.

"Morning, Marshal," the young man in the office said.

Hearing that, Clint rushed to the front of his cell once again and pressed his face against the bars. Sure enough, he spotted Marshal Packard entering the office and hanging up his coat like it was just another day at work.

"Marshal, I need to talk to you," Clint said, trying not to sound too aggressive.

The lawman glanced toward the cell with an expression

on his face that made it look as though that had put him out already. "What is it?"

"I'd like to know when I'm scheduled for trial."

"We'll see if that's necessary."

"Necessary? What are you talking about? It's my right."

"The way I see it, you gave up your rights the moment you decided to pull that gun of yours and start firing on innocent people."

"Innocent?" Clint said in disbelief. But rather than try to argue his case to two men who wanted to hear none of it, he decided to stick to his original point. "I need to tell my side of what happened. Is anyone interested in the truth or are you just set on watching someone swing?"

Marshal Packard walked slowly back to Clint's cell and stood in front of the bars with his arms crossed over his chest. "This town believes in doing things our way. We see justice done and we don't slow things up with unnecessary formalities. The judge is making his rounds today and when he gets to you, you can say your piece."

"And in the meantime, you'll just keep building those gallows?"

Packard looked in the direction of the hammering and smiled grimly. "I don't see any reason why not."

"That's a hell of a system you've got here."

"It works for us, Mister Adams. We like things nice and quiet here in Waylon City."

SEVENTEEN

The judge came by the marshal's office a little past lunch-time. There wasn't a clock anywhere that Clint could see and the watch that normally resided in his pocket had been taken away along with everything else on him during the confusion of the night before. The only way Clint knew it was past lunchtime was by the angle of the shadows and the scent of onions on the old man's breath.

Glaring at Clint through the bars like he was visiting a zoo, the judge listened to what Clint had to say without giving him more than a nod or two for acknowledgment. When Clint was done, the judge scribbled a few words on the book he used for taking notes and then got up from the stool that had been brought over for him.

"Is that all you have to say for yourself, Mister Adams?" the judge asked.

Clint felt as if he'd missed something very important, so he took a moment to think. Finally, he said, "No. I guess that's about it."

"Well, then I guess I'll be on my way. Good day to you, sir."

"Wait! Is that it? When's my trial?"

The judge only turned halfway in Clint's direction. He

looked as though he was afraid of getting dirty just by spending too much time that close to the cell. "I'm the acting judge here and I've collected my evidence. You'll be made aware of my decision when—"

"When what? When the noose slips over my head?"

"Please, Mister Adams. Such outbursts do not help your case."

Clint nodded, watching the older man carefully. More than once, the skills he'd picked up at the poker table had come through to save his life. Namely, the skill to read another man's face and gather useful information just by watching how they acted. Oftentimes, the important things were shown in the way another person reacted.

The judge had only listened to about half of what Clint had told him.

Not one word of Clint's story had even made a dent.

Whatever opinion the judge had coming into the marshal's office was the same one he took with him as he left.

Clint knew that much for certain.

Another thing he knew for sure was that he was to be hung the moment those workers outside had finished their hammering. Still, he needed to be completely sure about that before taking the next step.

After the judge had left and the door had shut behind him, Clint closed his eyes and listened for any and every noise he could possibly detect within the small building. Although it was hard to focus through the hammering, he was able to eventually weed out most of the sounds he knew to be coming from outside. From there, it was a simple matter of paying close attention to everything that remained.

"Marshal," Clint said while opening his eyes once more. "Are you still there?"

He heard the sound of footsteps as a man stepped out of one of the few blind spots Clint had from his vantage point. There was also the sound of another muffled voice that came from the spot that the footsteps had already left.

That told Clint that he'd been right in figuring there were two people left in the building now that the judge had gone. Marshal Packard walked toward the cell and stopped well out of arm's reach.

"What?" the lawman asked.

"Who did the judge talk to about what happened?"

Packard shrugged. "Whoever he needed to, I guess."

"Did he talk to the woman who owns the Ridgeway Inn? I was staying there and the owner can verify plenty of what I was saying."

"I doubt the judge talked to her. She's still pretty broken up about what happened to Emma. That girl was like a daughter to that nice lady, you know."

"Yeah. I also know I wasn't the one who shot her. The owner might have some pretty interesting things to say if anyone ever got around to asking her."

"I'd rather not bother her. She's got plenty on her plate already."

"Normally I'd agree. But seeing as how I'm about to get my neck stretched at any time here, I'd say time is of the essence." Clint fixed his eyes on Packard and saw that he was getting through to the lawman. "This is important, Marshal. If I'm right, you'll save yourself from hanging an innocent man. If I'm wrong, you'll only lose less than an hour of your time."

The other man in the building came from where he'd been sitting so Clint could see his face. It was the younger man who'd been there when Clint had woken up and he didn't look any friendlier this time around.

"I can go talk to her, Marshal," the younger man offered eagerly.

Perhaps the other man was a bit too eager, because Packard didn't look at all enthused about accepting the proposal.

Clint put just the right amount of doubt in his eyes when he looked at the marshal. It was the right amount, because it played off of the doubt the lawman was already expressing without pushing Packard too hard. Finally, the marshal shook his head and turned his back on the cell.

"No," Packard said. "I think I should be the one to talk to her. She is pretty worked up and might be a little hard to handle. You stay here and keep an eye on Mister Adams here."

Although Clint could read the lack of confidence the marshal had for his helper regarding that task, the younger man seemed perfectly oblivious to it. He was a bit disappointed in getting passed up for the job, but regained his enthusiasm when he took another look at the prisoner in his cell.

"All right, Marshal. I'll keep an eye on this here killer for ya."

Packard nodded, went to the coatrack by the door, and pulled on his jacket before stepping out into the cold. The wind gusted into the office, making him have to use some muscle to get the door closed, but he got it shut before too long.

Smirking at Clint, the younger man said, "Guess it's just you and me again. Just keep quiet and you won't have no troubles in there."

Clint nodded and threaded his arms through the bars. He kept his eyes on the other man.

"One down," Clint thought. "One to go."

EIGHTEEN

"So what the hell you lookin' at?"

The younger lawman was the only one besides Clint remaining inside the marshal's office. The lawman strutted toward the cell with his chest puffed out and a challenging look plastered upon his face. Anyone who didn't know any better might think the fresh-faced young man was Wyatt Earp himself.

But Clint did know better. In fact, he'd done his best to put that smug grimace upon the younger man's face as a way to boost that overly enraged ego of his. Such a thing was a flaw common to youth and Clint meant to get as much as he could out of it.

"What am I looking at?" Clint asked. "Not too much, if you ask me."

The younger lawman bristled at that and took another couple steps forward. "You've been eyeballing me ever since the marshal left. Is there some kind of problem?"

Clint shook his head, wearing just enough of a smile to stoke the fires inside the younger man. "Problem? Me? Oh no. Not at all."

"Good. Because I got a real quick way to solve your problems right here," the other man said, patting the holster at his hip. "It'd save the hangman some trouble, but we'd probably want to string you up anyway to give the folks around here something to look at. We all like a good hanging every now and then."

"Real tough talk coming from a man with a gun," Clint sneered. "Especially when he's talking to a man behind bars from way over there."

"What do you think I am?" the lawman asked, stepping up closer to the cell. "You think I'm stupid? You think I'll let you out of there so I can beat up on you some? I'll get plenty of chances for that when your time comes."

"Oh I'll bet. That should be perfect because that's when Marshal Packard will be here to cover your ass."

"You think I need him to handle the likes of you?"

Clint nodded.

"Just because you're some hot shit gunfighter, you think you scare me? You ain't nothing without that fancy iron of yours."

"I guess we'll never find out. The marshal doesn't even trust you to question some old lady, so it's probably best he leaves you behind for all the shit work."

The younger man was getting so angry, Clint could almost feel the rage boiling off of him. That was fine with him. In fact, Clint wouldn't have had it any other way.

"I do plenty around here," the younger lawman said as he took another step toward the cell. "Besides, what the hell do you know? You're just some killer who's about to get what's coming to him, just like the last two men that came through here got theirs."

"What two men?" Clint asked.

The young man smiled and nodded. "Oh, they was all tough just like you until they got themselves into a fight over some woman. Then they started throwing punches and one of them even got out a knife and cut Mister Adler right across the chest."

"Was it an accident?"

"Who cares? Mister Adler was just there watching the fight like everyone else when that knife came right across and sliced him."

"Did he die from it?"

"No, but them two troublemakers sure did. I watched them right in the cell next to you as they begged like little girls. They was still begging when they was hung, too. Just like you'll be begging when your time's up."

Clint didn't want to lose track of what he was doing, but he needed just a little more clarification. The point could have been very important to him considering his situation. "And all they did was accidentally cut someone in a fight?"

The younger man looked a bit put off by the question. "Mister Adler's still got the scar. Plus them two busted up half of Farrell's saloon when they was fighting."

That certainly was important. Knowing that extra bit of information not only told Clint he was justified in following through with his plan, but it told him he needed to move a bit faster than he already was. Putting on his game face once more, Clint locked his eyes on the younger lawman and put a sarcastic edge into his voice.

"Oh yeah," Clint said. "Taking care of those two scrappers really tested your mettle, didn't it? They sound like some tough customers."

"What? You think they weren't?"

"I think you probably got to kick them when they were down after Marshal Packard did all the tough work for you."

The younger man took another step forward and leaned toward Clint like a dog that was about to bite. "You best shut yer mouth."

"Or what? You'll cry to the marshal to come and scold me? You've got nothing over me except for the fact that I'm in this cell and you're not."

"Is that so? I sure as hell got one thing over you, mister, and it's right here," the lawman said, shifting himself forward another half step and patting the holstered revolver at his side. "Just make one more smart-ass comment and I'll drop you right in that cage."

"You're real brave, kid. Too bad it's all a bunch of talk."

The young man's eyes widened and he lunged forward with his fist clenched tightly and cocked back near his head. Clint stood his ground and waited for the punch to come as though he was watching the whole scene spool out before him in slow motion. At the last second, he knelt down and turned his head so he was out of the way of the other man's punch.

The incoming fist slammed noisily against the bars, accompanied by the sound of bones crunching beneath flesh. With the momentum of his punch combined with his own anxiousness to get his hands on the prisoner, the lawman's entire body was carried that much closer to the cell. His shoulder bumped against the bars and his feet struggled to maintain his balance.

Before the fist could be pulled away from the bars, Clint reached up and out to grab hold of it to make sure the lawman couldn't pull it back. With his other hand, Clint reached between the bars to make a straight line for his one true target.

The weight of the lawman's gun felt glorious in Clint's hand. Now that he had it, he flipped it around so he could grip it properly and then pulled the lawman tighter against the bars using the hand he still had in his grasp.

"All right now, listen closely, kid," Clint said, snapping the gun's hammer back for dramatic effect.

There were few sounds in the world that could grab someone's attention quicker than that distinctive metallic click. The younger man was no exception and when he heard that hammer snap back, his eyes widened into saucers and his entire body froze.

"You're going to unlock this cell door and let me walk out of here. You understand me?"

The young lawman nodded weakly.

"And while you're letting me out of here, you're going to move slowly and not do anything unexpected," Clint added. "Because this whole mess has made my hands a little on the shaky side." When he said that, Clint twitched the hand he used to hold the gun, which was the spark that got the younger man moving.

The keys were taken from his belt and the lawman opened the cell door without a bit of fuss. After that, Clint was a free man.

Of course, he was now also a fugitive.

NINETEEN

It wasn't Clint's intention to break the law. Hell, it wasn't even his intention to hurt the young lawman as he tied him down and gagged him with a section of cloth and a belt. But despite all of his good intentions, Clint sure as hell didn't intend on hanging for what happened to Tony Ackerman.

In the time he'd been in custody, Clint had heard plenty of words regarding Emma. Fortunately, none of them had been "killed" or "dead" so that gave him a bit of hope as far as she was concerned. The law in Waylon City was content to hang two men for a fistfight and the accidental cutting of some local, which told Clint a lot.

Mainly, it told him that he had no chance whatsoever in avoiding the noose himself. Then again, he'd been pretty much convinced of that fact after his farce of a trial. For all he knew, the judge that had come by to talk to him was actually some shopkeeper on his day off.

If he was going to get out of this with his name and neck intact, he was going to have to do it on his own. What he did may have been technically against the law, but Clint couldn't have felt any better as when he took his first step out of Marshal Packard's office.

He didn't worry about the younger lawman because he was tied right where he needed to be in order to buy Clint some precious time. What Clint was more concerned with was making his way through the town without drawing any attention to himself. To that end, he put on the coat and hat remaining on the rack by the door and kept his head down as he crossed the street.

The younger lawman was about the same size as Clint, so his hat and coat fit well enough to look like they belonged on their new owner. There was also enough room left over for the coat to hang nicely over the modified Colt that he'd reclaimed from the marshal's office and dropped back into its holster where it belonged. The clothes also weren't distinctive enough to stand out in anyone's mind. As Clint walked down the street, he did so like a single ant moving through a colony.

Like most other folks, the locals in Waylon City didn't talk to someone who looked like they weren't the sociable kind. People had their own matters to attend to and were perfectly content to let a man in a hurry keep right on walking.

The collar on his stolen coat flipped up to cover a good portion of his face, allowing Clint to make it almost back to the Ridgeway Inn before he was even noticed.

"Evenin'," one passerby said with an off-handed wave.

Clint gave a nod and grunted a syllable without breaking stride. The other person either didn't notice or didn't care. Whichever it was, Clint was happy for it and kept on moving. As much as he wanted to get out of town, there was something else more important that he had to see to.

That other task took him right where he shouldn't have been and in close proximity to the one man he needed to avoid more than anyone else in town. The Ridgeway Inn was just as quiet as when he'd first arrived and seemed even darker despite the fact that a slight trace of sunlight was peeking through a passing bank of clouds.

He waited until a solitary figure opened the door and walked out before making his move to get inside. Clint was already about to reach for the handle when he saw that the other person stepping out of the hotel was none other than Marshal Packard himself.

Clint sidestepped and turned his back on the lawman, all while making it seem as though he was studying something across the street. When he felt the other man walk out and stand on the boardwalk behind him, Clint thought for sure the marshal was going to draw his gun and confront him right then and there.

"You going inside?" Packard asked to the bundled up man standing with his back to him.

Clint shook his head impatiently and waved Packard off. "Waiting for my damn wife," he grunted before appearing to spot someone in the distance.

Clint couldn't tell what the marshal was doing, but the footsteps thumped away before too long. Taking a quick glance over his shoulder, Clint saw that Packard was indeed walking away, so he slipped into the hotel before the door could bang shut.

Standing behind the front desk was a skinny man whom Clint had never seen before. Judging by the flustered way he was looking over the papers piled in front of him, he wasn't too used to the job he'd been given. Clint walked past him while keeping the annoyed, distracted look upon his face.

That way, even though he couldn't see much from where he was standing, the man behind the desk wasn't too anxious to pursue any questions. He watched Clint walk through the lobby and head for the stairs. Although he'd been told to make sure anyone going up to the rooms had a good reason being there, he wasn't about to risk his neck for the policy.

The question was on the tip of his tongue. He knew

he needed to ask who the man was or even if he just needed help. From what he could see of those intense, burning eyes, none of those questions would have been suffered too lightly.

Clint let out the breath he'd been holding when he made it to the top of the stairs. He knew better than to relax, however, because he was still wandering about inside the lion's den and the sound of hammering could still be heard coming from down the street.

He entered his room, collected his things, and was out again in less than two minutes flat. From there, Clint walked down the stairs with his saddlebags slung over his shoulder as though it was the most natural thing in the world. There was still a more important matter to be handled and time was quickly running out.

It was in Clint's nature to take the occasional gamble when necessary. Some gambles, like the one he took now, were a lot bigger than others.

"I heard Emma Farraday was hurt last night," Clint said to the man behind the desk.

The skinny fellow nodded. "Oh yes. I'm filling in for her until she's well enough to return. Do you know her?"

"Yeah," Clint said, feeling better even though the other man's eyes were focusing on him a little too closely. "Pass on my best wishes to her."

"Who should I say is—" But the clerk stopped himself before finishing the question. The man in the coat was already gone.

TWENTY

Emma was still alive.

Just knowing that made Clint feel better. Leaving town without checking in with her wouldn't have been an option. No matter how many people were out to hang him, Clint simply couldn't have lived with himself if he hadn't set his eyes on hers one more time.

A man like Ackerman was going to get himself shot and killed on his own anyhow. A man like Clint was put into hot water practically on a monthly basis. But Emma was different. She was an innocent who'd gotten caught in the middle of some ugly business and Clint needed to know for sure just how badly she'd been hurt.

Still keeping his head down and his stolen coat wrapped tightly about himself, Clint left the hotel and walked toward the doctor's office. At least, it was the direction where the doctor's office had been the last time he was in town. He remembered it because it had been the town's doctor who'd brought him to Waylon City in the first place. It hadn't been any kind of special business. Just a matter of delivering a letter to the physician before the town had gotten their telegraph lines put in. Waylon City was so off the beaten path that mail only got delivered every couple of months, which was why Clint had been asked to make the delivery.

A lot had changed in town since then. Messages weren't so hard to come by, despite the fact that the town itself was still a far cry from the beaten path. Plenty of hands changed, but the town's leading physician had fortunately remained the same.

Clint spotted Doc Cohen through the window as he stood outside the same square little house that he'd visited the first time around. Unlike that first time, however, Clint didn't just walk straight up to the front door so he could knock and be let inside. He had to be a bit more careful this time.

Inside the little house, Doc Cohen was fussing over a table when he suddenly looked up at the very window where Clint had been standing. His instinct may have been on the money, but his speed wasn't quite what it once had been. Even so, he knew that someone had been looking through that window so he decided to have a look for himself.

He moved quickly for a man in his sixties, shuffling across the floor so his feet made noise like sandpaper across the wood. He stared through the glass and spotted a single figure about ten feet away. The figure lifted one arm and pointed toward the other side of the house before turning and walking that direction himself.

Cohen headed toward the other door on that side of the building, grabbing the rifle hanging over the mantel along the way. By the time he got to the side door and opened it, he had the rifle cocked and wedged under one arm.

"Someone out here?" Cohen asked the darkness.

His words hung in frozen wisps in front of his mouth and were quickly swallowed up by the cold air. Winter winds had a tendency of freezing away all the background sounds that one usually found outside. That made the noises that survived all the more prominent.

One of those noises was a set of footsteps crunching against cold gravel and chunks of nearly frozen dirt.

"Hello, Doc," came a familiar voice. "Remember me?"

Doc Cohen started to bring up the rifle, but lowered it the moment he got a good look at the face of the man wrapped up in that coat. He squinted his eyes and took a second glance just to be certain.

"Clint Adams? Is that you?"

Clint stepped forward and lifted his face high enough for it to catch a generous portion of light. "One and the same. Mind if I come inside? It's awfully cold out here."

"Of course. Come on in."

Clint stepped into the little house and let the bags he'd been carrying fall to the floor from where they'd been hidden beneath his coat. When he turned around, Doc Cohen was shutting the door and smirking back at him.

"I was starting to think you'd grown a hump," the doctor said.

Looking down at the bags, Clint couldn't help but start laughing. "It's nice to see a familiar face, Doc."

"Especially when you're wanted for murder?"

Clint's eyes snapped up and he wondered if he hadn't made a big mistake.

"Don't worry about me," Cohen said, setting the rifle down. "I think this town's sense of justice is on the skewed side. When I heard it was you that was accused of those terrible things, I knew the marshal had made a horrible mistake. I'm glad you got away."

"You know about that?"

"Well, I assume he didn't let you go. Not when they already went to all the trouble of building those gallows."

"I can't stay long, Doc. I had to come by to see if you knew anything about Emma. I was there when Ackerman shot her."

"I don't have anything to say about that, so why don't you just go ask her yourself?"

Clint looked in the direction Cohen was pointing and saw the little room with beds in it just down the hall. One of those beds was occupied by a slight, familiar figure. He couldn't rush to her fast enough and felt all his troubles lift when she looked back up at him and smiled.

"There you are," she said before wincing in pain.

"Are you all right?" Clint asked.

"It still hurts, but the doctor said I'll be fine."

Cohen stood in the doorway, looking over Clint's shoulder. "The bullet went right through and didn't hit any organs on the way. She's lucky."

Squeezing her hand, Clint added, "And I'm glad to hear that."

Emma looked up at Clint as though she was the one who needed to comfort him. "I told the judge what happened, Clint. I told him everything I could remember, but he wouldn't listen. He said I was delirious."

"He already had his verdict decided before walking in here," Cohen said. "Nobody disputed the fact that you shot that asshole Ackerman, so he just went through the motions when asking about Emma here. Tell you the truth, even if she hadn't hurt a hair on her head, you'd be in the same predicament."

Clint nodded. "I know."

"As much as I'd like to help you, I can't keep you here. I've got patients to think about and a business to—"

"Don't worry about all that," Clint interrupted. "Letting me see Emma was enough. Now I can do what I need to do with a clear head."

Still gripping Clint's hand, Emma pulled him down and gave him a kiss on the cheek. "I'll be fine. I'm just waiting for the stitches to heal."

Looking into her eyes, Clint could see that she was hurting, but not enough for anyone to worry too much.

The doctor was right about one thing, though. She'd been damn lucky to get away from that gunshot with just a nasty flesh wound.

On his way back to the side door, Clint stopped and picked up his saddlebags. Doc Cohen held out something from him clenched in a tight fist.

"Take this," Cohen said. "It's some money to get you by for a while."

"Don't need it, but thanks. I've got everything I need right here."

The doctor looked a bit uncomfortable as he said, "You mentioned doing what you needed to do. Should I ask what that might be?"

"No," Clint replied. "It'd be better if you didn't."

TWENTY-ONE

After tracking down his fair share of fugitives himself, Clint had become pretty good at figuring out how they managed to do what they did. That was the first step in tracking any beast, whether it walked on two legs or four, and it also gave him an insight as to what worked when on the run and what didn't. The danger in knowing too much about your prey was that you could too easily put yourself in their shoes.

On rare occasions, however, that wasn't such a bad thing.

One thing Clint had noticed when watching how a fugitive, or even a bank robber, operated was that a lot of what they did involved simple timing. Slipping through the fingers of a posse or hitting the most well-guarded of bank vaults relied heavily on acting quickly at just the right time and at just the right place.

There were chinks in all armor and holes in every net. That simple principle allowed Clint to not only get out of Waylon City, but also collect Eclipse before he left. All he had to do was pick a good spot to stay out of the way, watch for the comings and goings of the people nearby, and then move whenever an opening presented itself.

He didn't even need to hide. An empty corner served well enough and from there, he could even watch as the marshal passed by once or twice coming and going from his office. Clint smirked when he saw Packard walk by. Every time, the frustration on his face became more and more pronounced. At least that part of his plan was working better than expected.

Finally, the stableman left his barn unattended to catch a meal. That was when Clint slipped inside, saddled up Eclipse, and rode out of town. The only thing to mark that he'd been there was the small stack of money left in the stall where the Darley Arabian had previously been. There was enough to cover the stable fees as well as a little extra to foster some good faith.

He did attract a few glances as he rode out of town, but those were only from locals who looked just to see who was riding by. The marshal was on a different street at that particular moment. Once again, timing.

As soon as he put the town behind him, Clint felt like a new man. A part of him felt a little guilty as well because he'd gotten a taste of the freedom that must be so attractive to an outlaw. After being pushed around by the marshal, tossed into jail, and sentenced to hang, he'd broken out of that jail and ridden away thanks to his own prowess.

Normally, when he heard about jailbreaks, Clint's first thought was in putting the breaker right back into their cage. Now, having spent some time on the other side of that formula, Clint wondered how many others were right in breaking out of their cages to begin with.

As soon as that thought entered his mind, Clint tossed it straight back out again.

The jailbreaks he'd heard about were mostly because the men doing the breaking were notorious killers. After all, that was why their breaks had made front-page news or had become common knowledge in the first place.

Also, murder was a common part of most jailbreaks. That fact, alone, dissolved whatever empathy Clint might have felt for fugitives.

After all, he was able to do it without anyone getting hurt. Now that thought put a little smirk on Clint's face. As he touched his heels to Eclipse's sides, he wondered if Marshal Packard even knew what had happened.

TWENTY-TWO

The lawman made his rounds for the fourth time. Each time he retraced his steps around the town, he could feel the color in his cheeks becoming a deeper shade of red. This wasn't the first time something like this had happened, but it sure as hell was the most frustrating.

Trying not to appear so angry just because he didn't want to look like he'd lost control, Packard took a deep breath before stepping into the Broken Axle and let it out in a hiss. His attempt to appear in control fell apart, however, when he pushed the door open and slammed it shut behind him hard enough to rattle the walls.

The crowd wasn't its normal size, but pretty good considering the saloon had played host to a shooting death not too long ago. Every eye in that place turned Packard's way thanks to his entrance, but just as quickly turned back to what they'd been doing.

"Hey there, Marshal," the bartender said. "You sure I can't convince you to take a drink?"

The question was answered with an intense glare from Packard.

Wincing slightly, the bartender added, "Guess not. If you're here about Troy, I still haven't seen him."

89

A grizzled old man was sitting at one of the card tables that had been occupied by the same players for the last several hours. "What's the matter Marshal? You lose one of your deputies again?"

Packard took another deep breath and looked carefully around the room as he made his way to the card table. Not seeing any trace of his younger helper, the marshal focused all of his attention on the closest available target.

"What did you say, Tate?" Packard asked the old card player. "I don't think I quite heard you."

Old Man Tate glanced up at the marshal, thought about what he wanted to say, and then thought better about it. "Never mind."

"That's what I thought. Any of you seen Troy?"

There were grumbles and head shakes all around, none of which were positive.

"Jesus Christ," Packard muttered as he walked out of the saloon. The frustration was coming back and all of it was directed in the wrong place. He had a hanging to oversee and a killer in his custody. Not only that, but Tony Ackerman was set to be put in the ground the following day. That man may have been a pain in the ass, but he spent a lot of money, which went into the pockets of the town's businesses, and he was also a supporter of Marshal Packard himself.

With all those things on his plate, the lawman found himself being more upset at the very man whose sole purpose was to make his life easier. Now, Troy was nowhere to be found, which gave Packard yet another thing to occupy his precious time.

Frustrated, angry and getting more so by the second, Packard went back to his office so he could at least get off his feet for a few minutes. When he stepped inside, he heard the same thumping and mumbling that had been there a little while ago.

"Shut up, Adams!" Packard shouted. "What the hell's

got you so riled up anyway? I told you before, I don't got the time to cater to no killers so just sit in your cell and behave, goddammit!"

All he wanted to do was put his feet up and take a pull from the whiskey bottle he kept stashed in his bottom drawer. But ever since the visit from the judge earlier that day, his prisoner had been taking it upon himself to protest through a fit of noise and pounding. It wasn't the first time Packard had had to weather a caged man's tantrum, but he expected better from someone like Clint Adams.

The rattling and thumping continued. It sounded like the prisoner was just making noise and knocking his bed around, which was why the marshal had tried to avoid going back there. The last thing he wanted to do was clean up the cell when that was Troy's job in the first place.

Finally, the noise got to be too much and Packard was no longer able to block it out. Balling his fists, he stomped toward the cells in their corner at the rear of the office. "I told you too many times, Adams! Shut the hell—"

His words caught in his throat when he finally stood in front of the cell and took a closer look inside. The shape of the figure in there was about right, and he was still wrapped up under the sheet on the bed. The face, on the other hand, was not the one he'd been expecting.

"Troy? Is that you? Holy shit!"

Suddenly, the marshal's day got a whole lot worse.

TWENTY-THREE

Once he was well out of town, Clint knew he had two choices of where he could go from there. He could just keep riding and forget about going back to Waylon City ever again. That wasn't too difficult of a possibility since the town liked to keep to itself anyway and news of his escape might not go much farther than its boundaries.

His other choice was to clean up the mess that had been created around him so he could walk away with it all tied up nice and neat in his wake. That choice had a lot more involved, but Clint didn't really have to think too long to know that it was also the one he needed to pick.

Very seldom was the right thing to do the easiest. On a more practical note, Clint knew only too well that leaving behind unfinished business would always come back to haunt him. The last thing he needed was some ambitious lawman deciding to start doing his job by spreading the word about Clint's little scrape with lawlessness.

Even as he thought this through, Clint's body seemed to have already made up its mind. His mind was racing, but he'd brought Eclipse to a stop and was even turned around looking at the distant outline on the horizon that was Waylon City.

There was only one thing for him to do and that was to clear his name and set everything straight with the law before he found himself living as a fugitive for the rest of his life. Clint thought back to the moment that had changed everything for him and was amazed at how long ago it all seemed.

Emma may have been doing well, but Ackerman was still dead. Clint didn't have to check with anyone about that since he'd been the one to kill him. Just thinking about that brought the entire scene rushing back into his mind.

He could still hear Ackerman flapping his gums and spewing his insults. He could still hear Emma calling out for him. The gunshots still echoed in his memory, right along with the thump of lead punching into flesh and bone.

Suddenly, Clint recalled another little detail that had since become one of the most important to him. He hadn't been completely alone with Ackerman and Emma that night. There had been others on that street who'd watched the entire scene unfold.

Three others to be exact.

But recalling how anxious they'd been to get out once they knew they'd been seen, Clint figured those three wouldn't be too eager to share their insight. But eager or not, those were the men that Clint had to find. And if the looks on their faces at the time had told him anything, it was that they knew well enough to make themselves scarce.

Tracking them wasn't going to be easy. The difficulty factor increased even more considering that the trail he was after started in the one town that he needed to avoid the most. Getting out of Waylon City was one thing. Getting back in, snooping around, and leaving with his skin intact was another animal entirely.

Even knowing full well how hard a task it was going to be, Clint was eager to get started. Those other three men had seen everything as it happened. Of course, it also seemed that they were up to some bad business of their own, but that didn't change what they saw.

Finding them would be the only way to get enough evidence to clear his name. Finding a real judge would go a long way in that direction as well, but Clint figured he needed to take only one step at a time, especially when the first step could very well be off the side of a cliff.

Clint spent the entire next day camping and covering his tracks from the day before. He could tell that men were out looking for him, but they appeared to be more like hunters and cowboys rather than any sort of organized posse. For the time being, it seemed as though Marshal Packard wanted to try and find his prisoner on his own with what little resources his town had to offer for the task. That was just fine by Clint since he could have eluded those men for years if necessary.

Once again using timing to his advantage, Clint waited for the posse to head out for their daily search before going back into town himself. With the law away for the day, Clint had all the time he needed to take a look at whatever tracks had been left behind by the men who'd watched the last moments of Tony Ackerman.

As he figured, there wasn't much in the way of physical remains for him to follow. Clint thought back to that night and recalled where he'd spotted those three men and tried to get to that spot without being seen. It wasn't as hard as he imagined. The time of day combined with the general flow of foot traffic moving around him made it easy to simply keep his head down and blend into the background.

It wasn't until he stood in the spot that he decided was the same as where those three men had been standing that Clint realized an important bit of information. He was behind a stack of crates next to a small building, looking out at the front of the Broken Axle and imagining what the shooting must have looked like from there.

Clint stood up and turned around to leave, which was the moment he got a look at the same spot from another angle. Namely, he got a look at the building right next to him as well as the one not too far behind. The building next to the spot was a small tailor's shop and the one with a decent view of the spot was none other than Doctor Cohen's office. The doctor couldn't have watched the three men from his window, but he could have seen them leaving when they bolted out of there.

The tailor's shop was another promising lead. After all, if anyone was in there, they might have known if someone was skulking around right outside their shop. They might have also been potential witnesses to speak on Clint's behalf when the time came.

With the grim situation he was looking at, Clint figured that every little bit of help would count for a hell of a lot.

TWENTY-FOUR

Clint took a gamble when he went into that tailor's shop. Having someone there as a witness was a double-edged sword. If someone could speak up as to what had really happened, that person might very well be able to save Clint's neck. That same person might also recognize him from that same night and decide to call down the law and end Marshal Packard's hunt.

With the gallows completed and still standing not too far away from the marshal's office, Clint didn't feel too much in the mood to make that gamble. Unfortunately, he didn't really have much choice.

Clint walked into the tailor's shop, making sure to keep his jacket buttoned and the collar up to cover a good portion of his face. He puttered around a bit before making some small talk with the middle-aged woman working there.

"What's with the gallows I saw down the way?" Clint asked her.

The woman squinted at Clint for a moment and then turned to look out the front window as if she could see the gallows herself from there. She shook her head when she turned to look back at him. "Those were supposed to be for some man who shot Tony Ackerman in front of one of the saloons."

"Really? Do you know what happened there?"

"I heard someone moving about outside my store, but they was probably hiding. They ran out pretty quick once the shooting started."

"Can't say as I blame them," Clint said.

She shrugged. "I guess not." Suddenly, she smiled guiltily at Clint and said, "I was pretty frightened myself. When I heard those people running by this place, I thought it was one of the men doing the shooting."

"Was it?"

"No," she said while shaking her head. "At least I don't think it was. Probably some kids out too late. From what I hear, the marshal got one of the men right away. He was supposed to hang him today, but I guess they've put that off for a while."

Clint was going to say it was a shame to delay the hanging just so he could go along with the part he was playing of outside observer. He didn't think he could pull that off too believably, however. Even his poker face wasn't that good.

"I hear the law's looking for someone around here," Clint said. "You think it's one of those that were sneaking around outside this place?"

Her face paled and she turned to look toward the wall that butted up against that stack of crates. "Oh Lord, I hope not."

"Well, it sounded like whoever it is will be on the run for a while. I'm sure they're far from here."

Although she nodded at him, Clint doubted she took much comfort from his words. He let the matter drop after that and left the shop after buying a scarf and tipping his hat to the seamstress.

From there, he went to Doc Cohen's place. Clint was feeling more and more uncomfortable the longer he stayed in town. Although it appeared as though there wasn't a lawman left in Waylon City's limits, he learned long ago to trust his gut instincts when it came to such matters. To that end, Clint kept his head down and wrapped his new scarf around his face as an added measure.

When he got to the doctor's small office, he peeked through the window to see if there were any others inside with him. As before, not only was Doc Cohen alone, but he spotted Clint almost the moment his face appeared in the window.

After Clint tugged the scarf down from his face, he was waved toward the side door. Doc Cohen had the door open and held it open for him the moment he got there.

"Glad to see you're doing alright, Clint," the doctor said. "Although it might not be too wise for you to be here with Marshal Packard running the search for you and all."

"I didn't see too many faces I needed to worry about around here."

"True enough for now, but only for now. He'll stay out with some of his men for a while, but someone always comes back to check in here and get some more supplies and such."

That explained the uncomfortable feeling Clint had been getting. "Sounds like you've been keeping tabs on them for me."

Cohen nodded. "Mostly checking up on them without trying to look too suspicious myself. I wanted to see if I could find out what kind of posse would be coming after you. This whole thing is a debacle, Clint. If I could stop it, I would. I know you're no killer."

Clint patted the physician on the shoulder and told him, "It does me a lot of good just to hear someone say that. Thanks."

"No thanks are necessary. If I knew you'd be paying me another visit, I would have tried to find out more.

Truth is," Cohen added in a scolding tone, "I would've thought you'd have more sense than to come back into Waylon City under these circumstances."

"You know me, Doc. If I had any sense at all, I would still be building guns for a living. How's Emma?"

"She's resting in her own bed as of this afternoon. If you'd have been a couple hours earlier, you might have been able to see her. I wouldn't suggest it now, though."

"Don't worry about that. Even I know when not to push my luck." With that, Clint shook the doctor's hand and bundled his coat and scarf around him. "You didn't happen to see anyone running from the side of that tailor shop the night of the shooting did you?"

Cohen started nodding right away. "As a matter of fact, I did. I heard the shots and looked out my window to see if there was anyone coming to fetch me yet. I saw three men running from that vicinity as if their tails were on fire. I just figured they were spooked from the shooting."

"Do you remember which way they headed?"

"That way," Cohen said, hooking his thumb toward the back of the house. "I recognized one of their faces as Kyle Evans."

"Are you certain about that?"

"Oh yes. Kyle was a good friend of Tony's, which was why I wondered later on why he was so keen on getting away. He must have seen the shooting with his own two eyes." Suddenly, Cohen blinked and cocked his head to one side. "Do you think that's important?"

TWENTY-FIVE

With the uneasiness gnawing away at the inside of Clint's belly, he quickened his steps the moment he was outside the doctor's office. It was the time of year when the daylight hours were few and far between, so the sky was already turning into a smear of dark red and purple.

In that respect, the elements were in Clint's favor because the sun was at an angle so that it shot directly into the eyes of anyone looking to the west. Keeping that well in mind, Clint hurried back to where he'd tethered Eclipse and tried to look unaffected by the rumble of other approaching horses.

After climbing into the saddle, Clint pointed the Darley Arabian toward the brilliant sunset and flicked the reins. The last time he'd ridden out of town, he'd promised not to come back until he could clear his name. Sometimes breaking a vow like that was unavoidable, and other times it was just plain stupid.

This time had been unavoidable.

A next time would be stupid.

Considering what he'd gained from this last visit, however, Clint was inclined to overlook the possible disaster it could have been. Not only had he verified the presence

100

of those three men he'd spotted at the shooting, but he got the direction they'd headed afterward and a name to go with one of the faces. All in all, not a bad way to spend the day.

And just when he thought he was far enough away from town to ease up on the reins a bit, Clint heard the familiar rumble of other horses running in a pack that he'd heard not too long ago. It was the posse. Clint didn't need to get a close look at who was riding in the saddles to know that the group of horses belonged to the lawmen pursuing him.

Waylon City wasn't well known enough for such large groups to come by on a frequent basis and that posse was the only large group of riders that Clint knew for sure was in the area. Using his ears along with a quick glance over his shoulder, he gauged the distance between himself and the riders in a matter of seconds.

The others were just under a mile away. At least, that was a close enough guess to suit his purposes. Considering the rocky terrain and sloping hills that served to keep the town so well hidden, it wasn't too big of a surprise that the riders could get so close to him before Clint knew.

He angled Eclipse's direction slightly so he could steer away from the riders while still keeping himself pointed toward the sunset. Knowing it would look suspicious for him to turn away like that and race off, Clint got Eclipse going fast enough to lose the posse without drawing more attention his way.

It was difficult for Clint to pick a spot as a destination. He was familiar with the area in a general way, but didn't have intimate knowledge of every nook and cranny. Also, that blazing sunset took away as much from his own field of vision as it did to anyone trying to ride in his wake.

When Clint took another look over his shoulder, it took

a moment for his eyes to adjust. Once his eyes did adjust, he wasn't too happy with what he found.

"Aw hell," he grunted to himself.

Marshal Packard had been riding constantly ever since Clint had escaped from his jail cell. Whenever he got tired or felt as though he might as well call for help from other lawmen in the area, Packard thought ahead to what those lawmen would say when they asked why he needed that help. He thought about what he would say to any of the people in town when they asked how the search was going or why it was needed in the first place.

The answer to all of those questions led inevitably to the one thing he didn't want to say to another living soul. Clint Adams had gotten away because he'd pulled the wool over Packard's eyes. And the reason he'd gotten such a head start was because Adams had managed to keep that wool over Packard's eyes for way too long.

Every minute counted when it came to that first half hour after Clint Adams had managed to get that door open. Every minute at the beginning of the escape bought him precious time and allowed him to get farther away before he was missed.

Thinking back to how many times Packard had glanced at that cell and assumed the figure squirming in that bed was Clint Adams just made the lawman wince. Even before he'd gotten Troy out of there, Packard had had the young man swear not to mention what had happened to him again.

Ever.

Now, he felt that every moment he spent personally chasing Adams down was like paying penance for his own stupidity. He would leave no stone unturned and would ride up and down every pass until he either found Adams himself or some trace that would lead to him. Nothing would stop him. Not hunger, not thirst, and not even his own desire to get some rest and close his eyes for a couple of hours.

During the ride back toward town, Packard was constantly on the lookout for any sign of his target. Even though he knew better than to think that Adams would be foolish enough to go back into town, Packard kept his eyes peeled. They'd been peeled so long, in fact, that he almost doubted them when he actually spotted something.

"Allan," Packard said to one of the nearby members of his posse. "Take a look right there."

Moving his horse up alongside the lawman, Allan squinted into the sun at the spot where Packard was pointing. "What am I looking at, Marshal?"

"On the horizon. Right there."

Suddenly, Allan started to nod. "Oh yeah. Looks like someone's out there."

"Go check it out."

"But we were headed back into town for some fo—"

"If you're not back soon, someone will bring you your dinner. Right now, I want you to go and check out that rider. If you need any help, just fire a shot and we'll come after you."

Keeping the rest of his complaints to himself, Allan snapped his reins and got his horse running in a straight line toward that other rider.

TWENTY-SIX

Clint had been hoping to steer clear of the posse for a little while longer. It would have been too much to ask to keep away from them completely, especially since he wasn't working just to escape the searchers. But no matter how easy it was to avoid them, that didn't make being spotted any less tricky.

He'd cursed when he first saw one of the posse members break away from the pack and start galloping his way. He cursed again when he saw what appeared to be movement from the rest of the posse soon after that first one had split off. Clint had every bit of faith in his and Eclipse's ability to get away from the lawmen. He cursed mainly because it had been his own dumb fault for getting close enough to be spotted in the first place.

The trail that Clint rode was on a rugged slope that led up into some steep hills with a river running at the bottom of a drop that was at least seventy-five feet deep. Although he wasn't in the mountains per se, Clint was close enough to them to feel the pressure in his ears as Eclipse took him higher up. Behind him, Waylon City lay in its protective nook with mountains on one side and an expanse of barren land on the other.

In front of him, Clint could see much more promising terrain. There was a twisting path that cut off of the main trail and led farther up into the rocky hills. As he followed the path with his eyes, he noticed that there were enough twists and turns for him to find some shelter and find it fast.

Pulling back on the reins, Clint slowed Eclipse down a bit so the Darley Arabian wouldn't lose his footing while turning onto the smaller path. Like any great horse, Eclipse thought one step ahead of his rider and instinctually headed for the new path the moment he caught sight of it. All Clint had to do was give the occasional nudge in the right direction, hunker down, and hang on as Eclipse climbed into the rocks.

Clint took a look back in the direction of the posse and saw that the one member who'd split off from the rest was closing in fast. His horse was running at a full gallop and would be there in only a minute or two. Having sacrificed speed for climbing, Clint knew that he'd committed himself to his current course since it was too late to think about outrunning the posse. He also knew that the terrain flattened out on the other side of the hills, which would make that a more dangerous choice for someone who preferred to remain unseen.

Eclipse was doing pretty well considering he was built more for speed and stamina instead of navigating through tight crags and steep inclines. He was no pack mule, but neither was the horse that thundered past the turnoff that Clint had taken not too long ago himself.

Clint had heard the approaching hooves beating against the packed ground. Due to the close quarters and the rocky walls closing in around him as he went up, those noises bounced around too much for him to guess how far away their source could have been. He didn't have to guess anymore, though. The horse that had been chasing him was in sight.

What troubled him more than that was the fact that that same horse was turning around and headed back toward the path that branched up toward the higher ground. As the member of the posse came to a stop at the turnoff, he looked up along the path until his eyes inevitably found Clint's position.

"I'll be damned," Allan said in words that bounced among the rocks until they reached Clint's ears. "It's you!"

Clint saw the other man tugging a rifle from the holster on the side of his saddle. Fighting back the instinct to draw his modified Colt, Clint reminded himself that even if the other man wasn't a lawman himself, he was acting in the name of the law. For that reason alone, he knew he couldn't hurt him.

Unfortunately, no member of the posse was going to feel quite so charitable when they got their sights on him. If Clint needed any proof of that, he just needed to watch Allan draw his rifle and lever a round into the chamber with a wide, expectant smile on his face.

The sound of the lever ratcheting within the rifle clattered among the rocks. It rattled Clint down to his bones, butting solidly against his resolve to not shoot any of the lawmen under any circumstances. Even though he could have easily drawn and taken a shot before the posse member fired that rifle, Clint gritted his teeth and dropped his body down low over Eclipse's neck.

On the path below, Allan sighted down the rifle's barrel and cursed under his breath when his target suddenly fell from sight. A second ago, he'd had Clint's head and upper body as a prime target, but now the only thing he could see was the occasional flicker of black as the stallion's head churned back and forth with every step.

Allan thought about firing his rifle into the air to alert Marshal Packard, but Clint was close to getting on the other side of the outcropping and would be gone before the others could get there. Besides that, it would look much better for him if Allan could run down and corner Clint Adams on his own. He would even be entitled to a bigger cut of the reward.

Once again, Allan smiled as he steered his own horse onto the alternate path and started the zigzagging climb for himself.

Farther up the path, Clint was only starting to feel his shoulders come down from around his ears when he realized that the posse member wasn't going to shoot at him after all. Well, he wasn't going to shoot for the moment, anyway. That would have to be enough comfort and Clint focused his attention on trying to get away from the other man completely.

After clearing a steep rise, the trail widened a bit and appeared to lead out of the rocks. With the man behind him picking his way along the tricky climb, Clint figured that if he could break free and get Eclipse running fast enough, he might just be able to leave the posse in the dust.

With the taste of victory on the tip of his tongue, Clint was just about to snap his reins when he got a better look at the path directly in front of Eclipse. It led out of the rocks, sure enough. The bad news was that it led out of the rocks and into empty space.

Clint pulled back on the reins with enough force to drag Eclipse's head all the way to one side. Although extreme, the strong tug was just enough to stop the Darley Arabian before he charged so close to the edge that a fall would be unavoidable. Several small stones that had been loosened by Eclipse's hooves rattled forward and toppled over the edge to clatter on the ground about sixty feet below.

Before Clint could feel too relieved about the spill he'd avoided, the sound of charging hooves came from the path behind him.

TWENTY-SEVEN

Clint saw the other horse coming and immediately knew there was going to be trouble. Even as he was twisting around to get a better look at the approaching rider, Clint was swinging his foot over Eclipse's back so he could drop down from the saddle. His heart was slamming inside his chest and the blood was pumping so furiously that it sounded like a flood in his ears.

Already, the other man was close enough for Clint to get a good look at his face. The posse member's eyes were widening with fear as his hands struggled desperately to pull back on the reins hard enough for his horse to obey.

Clint could see the animal's eyes as well and those were more telling than those of its rider. The horse had that glazed-over look in its eyes that betrayed a mixture of excitement and panic within the beast. That look was familiar to any man who rode horses and it was something that was to be avoided whenever possible.

There wasn't enough time for Clint to think everything through. With the other horse barreling toward him as well as toward the drop-off, he had just enough time to think about where his next step or two would be. Any

further than that, and he was in danger of forcing himself
to hold back, which could very well be a mistake that
would cost everyone dearly.

Clint ran toward the oncoming horse as his hand
flashed down to the Colt at his side. In a fluid, natural
motion, he drew the weapon and pointed it upward. His
finger was already squeezing the trigger as the barrel
sighted first toward the horse's head and then at the
rider's. Finally, the gun was pointed straight into the sky
and that was when the shot exploded from the cylinder.

Amid the rocks, the gunshot sounded like it had been
fired from a cannon. It was so loud that it startled Eclipse,
who had become very used to such sudden noises after
spending so much time around Clint. More importantly,
the gunshot startled Allan's horse. That animal was startled so much, in fact, that it reared slightly and turned
sharply away from the source of the thunder.

That sudden motion shifted the posse member in his
saddle. The man's momentum kept him moving forward,
even though the beast beneath him had already turned
about ninety degrees to the right. The result was simple:
the stronger of the two was the horse, so that was the one
that completed the turn. Allan slid right out of his saddle
and landed on his stomach upon the ground.

Clint could see what was going to happen the moment
that horse veered off and away from the edge. He tried to
run back so he could offer a hand to the falling man, but
his body was simply unable to keep up with his racing
mind. Clint's hand reflexively holstered the Colt and
reached out toward the posse member, but was unable to
do any good before the other man hit the ground.

As soon as his body slammed against the dirt, all of
the breath rushed out of his lungs. His face twisted in a
pained grimace, which quickly became an expression of
utter surprise. The horse was galloping back down the
path, but he was still moving in the direction that had

gotten him in so much trouble in the first place.

Dirt and gravel crunched beneath his chest and stomach. Allan kicked at the ground, but he still kept sliding toward the drop-off. As he did, he thought back to the vague warnings he'd gotten from the marshal about the tricky terrain. The truth of the matter was that the men of the posse were settlers and not as familiar with every last inch of the surrounding area.

Well this member of the posse was getting educated in the dangers of the terrain real quickly. Unfortunately, he only had about another fraction of a second before that education sent him tumbling down to a steep graduation.

Now completely consumed by panic, the posse member's eyes no longer saw much of anything but the rush of dirt and rock sailing past him. His feet were dangling out into empty space and his knees had just slid over the edge as well. His arms were flailing desperately for anything to grab on to, and just when he thought he wasn't going to find anything to stop him from falling, one hand closed around something solid.

Clint gritted his teeth and let out a pained grunt as his arm was nearly wrenched from its socket. It was only because of his quick reflexes that he was able to snap his hand forward and take hold of the other man's wrist with less than half a second to spare. The grab was just as fast as any quick-draw, but with one big difference; this time instead of taking a life, he'd saved one.

"Stop kicking," Clint shouted as he tightened his grip and tried to plant his feet a little deeper into the ground. "Just settle down and let me pull you up."

But Allan was still thrashing at the end of Clint's hand, his entire body responding as though he was free-falling through empty air.

Clint knew the other man was scared and not thinking straight. Unfortunately, that didn't help him pull Allan up any quicker. So rather than try to fight against the other man's panic, Clint held on and just let him dangle for another couple of seconds until Allan realized he was no longer dropping.

Finally, Allan's eyes cleared and he looked up at Clint as though he didn't quite know what was going on. It didn't take him long to figure it out, and when he did, his body stopped its violent fits. At that moment, a calm seemed to flow over him like a cool breeze. He looked up at Clint and blinked several times as though he'd just awoken from a dream.

"Wh . . . what?" was all Allan could manage to say.

Despite the fact that it was easier to keep his grip when the other man stopped kicking, Clint still didn't think Allan was getting any lighter.

Pulling in a breath, Clint smirked and said, "It would be a whole lot easier if you could help me out here."

That woke the posse member up for good and got Allan to start climbing back up to the ledge.

TWENTY-EIGHT

Clint fought through the pain in his shoulder and hauled the posse member back onto the edge of the drop-off. Once Allan was safely on the path, Clint stepped back and tried to sum up the damage that had been done to his arm in the process.

From what he could tell, the shoulder had almost been pulled from its joint. When he swung his arm back and forth, it sent shards of pain through that entire side of his body. The more he moved it, however, the more bearable the pain became.

"You alright?" Allan asked, scooting carefully back and away from Clint. His hand drifted toward his gun, but only hovered over the holster rather than trying to make a genuine grab for the weapon.

Stepping back and rubbing his shoulder, Clint nodded and replied, "It's not too bad." He was about to say something else, but Clint stopped himself before another word could escape his lips. Suddenly, he was aware that he was on one side of the law looking down at a man who sat squarely on the other.

Allan was aware of that same thing himself. That much was evident by the way his expression shifted slowly from relief to a guarded wariness. His eyes darted back and forth, surveying his surroundings and trying to come up with a quick summation of his situation.

His horse had stopped running and could be seen wandering back up the path toward him. The animal was moseying slowly, however, and was nowhere close enough to be of any help should the need arise. Allan's hand drifted toward his holster again and so far it seemed as though the motion had gone unnoticed.

Clint smirked when he saw the posse member's fingers finally come in contact with the leather gun belt. "You won't find what you're looking for there," he said to Allan. "But you might want to try looking over the edge."

Allan's heart skipped a beat and stopped completely when his palm slapped against an empty holster. Without stopping to think about putting his back to a potential enemy, he twisted around to look over the edge as Clint had suggested. He didn't see his gun anywhere down there, but he couldn't see it anywhere nearby either.

Another wave of panic flooded through his system when he swung his upper body back around to get a look at the fugitive he'd been chasing. Allan's mind filled with possible endings to that turn, most of which included him staring down the barrel of Clint's gun.

But when he got his eyes turned back to face Clint, he wasn't looking down the barrel of any gun. In fact, he was still looking at the same smirk that had been there before. The smile was a little uncomfortable as well, but it was a far cry from anything that the posse member needed to worry about.

"What about you?" Clint asked. "Are you hurt?"

Allan shook his head. He still felt stunned after all that had happened. But more than that, he was having a hard time figuring out the man that had just saved him from a cartload of injuries and maybe even death itself.

"I'll be alright," Allan replied. The fact of the matter

was that nearly every part of him hurt to one degree or another. Every single bit of pain, however, was a hell of a lot better than it might have been.

Suddenly, Allan's eyes shot open and he decided what needed to be done about Clint Adams. "That shot you fired," Allan said quickly. "Marshal Packard would have heard that. He'll be on his way right now with the rest of his men."

Clint straightened up and lifted his head slightly to the wind. The pain in his shoulder was forgotten the moment he heard the distant rumble of approaching horses.

Allan struggled to his feet, wincing now and then at the stabs of pain he felt throughout a good portion of his body. Dusting himself off and checking on the location of his wandering horse, he said, "I was supposed to fire a shot if I needed help," he said as though he'd just remembered and even regretted the policy. "The marshal told me he'd send help the second he heard it. I don't know how long it's been, but I'd say that there isn't much time before he and the others will . . ."

Allan trailed off when he turned his head back in the direction that Clint had last been. But Clint was no longer standing in that spot. Instead, he'd already called his horse to him and was settling into his saddle. As his eyes fell upon the Colt hanging at Clint's side, Allan felt another pang of fear stab him in the gut.

"Collect your horse and go meet your marshal," Clint said sternly. "And do yourself a favor."

The fear in Allan's gut flared up a bit more as he awaited the threat that was surely on its way.

"Watch yourself on these paths," Clint said, rather than the harsher words Allan had been expecting. "Next time, you might not be so lucky."

And with that, Clint flicked his reins to get Eclipse moving back down the path. He left behind him a nervous horse and a man who was in no big hurry to rejoin his posse.

A couple minutes later, Marshal Packard and most of his posse came racing up to the place where the trail branched off to lead up into the rocks. He searched the area around him while holding up a hand to signal for the others to come to a stop.

"We can't let up now, Marshal," one of the others said. "Allan could be in trouble."

Everyone but the marshal himself was panting as though they'd run the entire way on their own two feet. Packard glanced around at them more as a way to shut them up rather than acknowledge what was being said.

"The shot came from here," Packard said. "If we ride much farther, we may just pass him up."

There were nods all around as the rest of the men took in that bit of common sense. Seeing that only made Packard more resentful of the fact that he only had a pool of shopkeepers and old ranchers to pull from when it was time to form a posse.

Standing up in his stirrups, Marshal Packard turned his head around in a wide arc as he shouted out, "Allan!? You around here? Let us know where you are!"

One of the posse members started stabbing his finger toward the horizon farther up the trail. "I see someone riding away, Marshal. Maybe it's him."

Before Packard could turn to get a better look, he heard a voice answering his call from up in the rocks.

"I'm right here, Marshal," Allan hollered.

Everyone looked in that direction and saw Allan come limping down the path leading his horse by the reins.

"Jesus, Allan, you look like hell," Packard said. "What happened up there?"

Allan paused and looked up into the rocks from which he'd came. "Got thrown from my horse."

"What about that shot that was fired?"

Again, the limping member of the posse paused and then shrugged. "Misfire."

The rest of the posse seemed relieved and a few even climbed down from their saddles to make sure Allan was alright. Marshal Packard, on the other hand, didn't seem relieved at all. He eyed Allan suspiciously before turning to look at the figure in the distance that had been pointed out earlier and had since been forgotten.

"Son of a bitch," Packard grumbled under his breath.

TWENTY-NINE

This time, when Clint put Waylon City behind him, he kept it there. After leaving the marshal's posse behind, Clint let Eclipse run full-out for the better part of a day. The Darley Arabian loved the vigorous run and tore up the miles like he had a personal stake in the matter. Clint enjoyed a fast ride himself, so he hung on and just let the stallion do what he was put on the earth to do.

He headed south, following the leads he'd gotten from his second trip into town. Now that he had a name and direction to use as a jumping-off point, Clint felt confident that he could track down at least one of the three men he was after. Leaving Waylon City in a cloud of dust had another advantage as well: it kept him out of Marshal Packard's immediate reach.

On one hand, Clint could fully appreciate the fact that the lawman was trying to do his job. On the other hand, he wasn't doing his job very well if it took so little to allow an innocent man to hang. In fact, the more he thought about it, the madder Clint felt toward Packard.

How many other so-called trials had gone exactly like his?

How many other innocent men had paid the ultimate

price simply because they weren't able to break out of their cells before it was too late?

Rather than stew very long on the subject, Clint simply snapped his reins and kept riding south. At least he was content in the knowledge that he'd done the right thing in getting out of jail.

He didn't stop too many times during the day. Eclipse really didn't seem to need many breaks and Clint was perfectly content to get as far away as quickly as possible. During one of their few rest periods, Clint climbed down from the saddle and started digging around in the bags slung over Eclipse's back.

They were on a high point in the trail with tufts of grass poking out of the cold, packed earth on either side. The wide-open land sprawled out in every direction, which was one of the reasons Clint had chosen that particular spot. After a minute or two of searching through the saddlebags, Clint found what he'd been looking for.

The spyglass was made out of dented metal and chipped glass. Despite the wear, the instrument worked just fine and had served him well throughout many years. Clint lifted the smaller lens to his eye and searched the tract of land he'd left behind.

Miles of trail disappeared in an instant as he peered through the glass. As he panned from one side of the horizon to the next, Clint couldn't spot a single other rider. He checked again just to be sure, but all he came up with were a few dust clouds that had been kicked up several miles away. It could have been the posse, but they didn't come into view even after he sat there and waited to see them.

Nodding, he collapsed the spyglass and placed it back into his saddlebag. Perhaps he'd lost the posse on his own or perhaps they'd decided to keep close to their own town. After seeing the posse in action, Clint figured they could also just be so inept that they allowed him to get away without meaning to.

As he thought of those things, Clint remembered the expression on that one posse member's face as he was pulled up after nearly falling off that ledge. There had been fear and surprise in those eyes, to be sure. But more than any of that, Clint recalled there being a good amount of gratitude as well.

That left the possibility that the posse member was showing that gratitude by steering the others away from Clint's trail. Clint couldn't exactly hope for too much help in that direction, but any small amount of distraction could do him a world of good.

Since there was no way for him to know for sure what kept the posse so far back, Clint decided to enjoy it for what it was and keep on going. Any man who didn't know how to savor whatever good fortune came his way usually didn't get much more.

After stretching his legs and allowing Eclipse to rest his for a spell, Clint saddled up and continued his ride south.

For the moment, it didn't really matter much whether the posse was slow, stupid, or just looking in the wrong place. It didn't even matter whether or not the man Clint had saved had had a bout of conscience, which was what granted him some extra time to get away.

It didn't matter whether or not Marshal Packard was going to seek help from other lawmen in other parts of the state. For the time being, there was only one thing that did matter to Clint: the fact that there were only a limited number of towns within a reasonable distance south of Waylon City.

Whoever had watched Ackerman try to kill Clint and Emma and then ran away only had a few places they could go. They couldn't live off the land forever and when they did pull back into civilization, Clint would be right there to greet them.

THIRTY

It had been one week since Clint had raced his way through those rocks with the posse hot on his heels. In that time, he'd barely allowed himself a decent night's rest so he could keep on riding and finding the trail of those three men who were his only real witnesses.

Not only had those three men seen the fight between Clint and Ackerman for what it was, they were more than likely wrapped up in it themselves. The more time Clint had to think it over, the more convinced he became of that very fact. The only thing he needed to do was find them so he could piece together what they were doing hiding out in those shadows in the first place.

With each day that passed, the chill in the air became sharper and more relentless. Every so often, the bitter winds would carry snow on their backs, which felt like little daggers slicing into Clint's face as he rode on. It seemed as though Nature herself was gnashing her teeth at the conflict between Clint and the posse chasing him down.

And there was no denying the fact that Packard and his men were still indeed gunning for Clint. Even though he didn't see much of the posse that first day or so, Clint caught plenty of glimpses of them sniffing around several miles behind him or even thundering past him while he and Eclipse tucked themselves away in a cave or gully somewhere.

He'd spotted the town some time ago, and it was the first real settled area in the rugged land south of Waylon City. After giving Packard a bit of time to spot the town as well, search through it, and move on, Clint steered Eclipse toward the clump of scattered buildings and took yet another gamble by riding straight down the main street.

According to a splintered sign just outside of town, the place was called Arrowhead Creek. Clint knew he'd crossed down into Wyoming, so that at least solved the mystery of where he was. Too bad there were still plenty more mysteries lined up behind that first one.

Arrowhead Creek appeared to be about the same size as Waylon City. Towns in that part of the country tended to keep themselves fairly small. They were either stuck up in or amid the mountains or in the middle of so much empty space that the wind itself threatened to blow away whatever was built there.

The truth of the matter was that there simply wasn't enough nearby to attract enough people to populate a major city. Ranchers tended to keep to themselves. Cowboys came and went with their herds. And most other folks were more intent on getting themselves into Canada, California, Oregon, or any number of places that seemed more attractive for one reason or another.

As Clint rode into town, he didn't have to work too hard to keep people from looking at him more than a moment or two. The plain truth was that after several days of living off the land and sleeping on the cold hard ground, he wasn't much to look at.

Clint's eyes reflected every one of those rough nights spent out in the elements. His face was haggard and cov-

ered with dark bristles and his skin looked like rawhide
that had been left in the rain and forgotten. Since he didn't
feel much better than he looked, all Clint had to do was
return someone's glance for that person to quickly look
away.

Fortunately, there weren't very many people out and
about the night that Clint arrived in Arrowhead Creek. At
least that way, only those few he did see could tell anyone
else about the grizzled figure that had come plodding into
town like something being dragged behind a cat.

Clint normally liked to treat himself to a good hotel
room after spending enough time in the elements. This
time was different, however. This time, Clint wasn't too
concerned about creature comforts and was more focused
on getting his job done quickly and correctly. For that
reason, he rode straight past the one hotel he spotted and
made his way to the biggest saloon instead.

Bigger saloons were more likely to have rooms to rent
out to their customers. And saloon owners were less likely
to ask many questions of the people that rented those
rooms, since they were oftentimes drunk, disorderly, or
both. Clint also knew he had a better chance in finding
the information he needed from a place like the Double
Barrel Saloon.

The Double Barrel was the second saloon Clint found
as he rode down the street, and it was also the largest. It
was about the size of a small hotel, but sported two floors
and a balcony overlooking the main street. What clenched
the deal, however, wasn't anything so cunning on Clint's
part. It was the smell of frying bacon wafting out of the
saloon's doors to grab Clint by the nose like an invisible
hand.

After tying Eclipse to a post outside the place, Clint
stepped into the saloon amid a swirl of snow kicked up
by a rowdy wind. That wind slammed the door shut be-

hind him, announcing his presence better than a shot fired in the air.

"Rough night out there, ain't it?" the barkeep asked from behind a row of disinterested drinkers.

Dusting off his shoulders, Clint stepped up to the bar and shook the frozen flakes from his hat. "I'll say it is. You got anything back there to warm me up?"

At that point, the barkeep stepped up closer to where Clint was standing. Clint had thought the bartender's voice was a bit high, but he'd also heard it through a gust of wind blowing in his ears. Now that he saw who'd done the speaking, he knew his first instinct was dead-on.

The bartender's voice wasn't actually that high. Especially since it was coming from a woman. Clint's face must have still shown a bit of surprise, because the barkeep laughed a bit at his reaction as she set a glass down in front of him.

"You're new in town," she said simply while pouring a generous shot of whiskey into Clint's glass.

"Actually, I was thinking of something more along the lines of coffee."

"And I was thinking I'd just be looking at the same old men that normally come in here," the barkeep retorted. "Looks like we both got ourselves a nice little surprise this evening."

Clint returned her smile and nodded. Feeling another jolt of cold rip through him, he lifted his glass and said, "What the hell. Here's to pleasant surprises."

THIRTY-ONE

A good portion of the Double Barrel Saloon was taken up with the tables and chairs scattered around the single room. That room wasn't very big, which explained why the three customers that were already in there made the place feel more crowded than it actually was. A big fireplace took up one wall and was framed by a rugged stone hearth. The bar itself was a simple boxy structure that came up to between Clint's waist and chest.

What caught Clint's interest more than the bar or any of the other pieces of furniture was the woman who stood behind that bar. Her hair was cut short, but not too short. It fell against the sides of her face and sprouted in the occasional tuft in a way that made her eyes seem to be always glinting with a mischievous light.

Her skin was the color of lightly creamed coffee and seemed to be every bit as smooth. Watching Clint carefully with dark, rich brown eyes, she waited for him to drink his whiskey and set the glass back onto the bar before reaching out once again with the bottle. "First one's free for all handsome newcomers in town," she said. "Care for another?"

Not a big lover of whiskey, Clint still couldn't dispute

the fact that the firewater did an awfully good job of thawing him from the inside out. Even so, he shook his head and said, "Make it a coffee and you've got yourself a deal."

The bartender stuck her full bottom lip out in a teasing pout. "Was it something I said?"

"No. I'm just worried about you trying to get me drunk just so I lower my defenses."

"Honey, if I wanted to get closer to you, this bottle is the last thing I'd need."

The other customers were all older men who resembled a group of down-on-their-luck miners. Not one of those weathered faces showed the first hint of a smirk at the bartender's sexy voice or quick wit. Like people who'd lived their whole lives at the foot of an awe-inspiring mountain range, they'd simply grown accustomed to the view.

"I'll still pass on the whiskey," Clint said. "But I did smell something cooking in here. Is there any of it left?"

At first, she didn't seem to know what he could be talking about. Then, glancing over her shoulder toward a narrow door behind the bar, she said, "I don't serve meals here. I was just putting together something to fill my stomach."

"Well make a plate for me and you can charge me for three shots of whiskey. How does that sound?"

"Sounds like you may be used to eating in some cheap places, but then again I'm not much of a cook. You got yourself a deal." Turning to look around at the rest of her customers, she asked, "Does anyone need anything before I try my hand at serving food?"

"Yeah," came a gravelly voice from the back of the room. "A bucket and mop to clean up once that fella gets a taste of that slop you call food."

There was a round of agreements to that statement, all of which were shaken off by the bartender as she turned

her back on them and headed for the next room. When
she opened the narrow door behind the bar, she filled the
air with the same smells that had brought Clint in from
the cold.

His mouth practically watered at the scent of bacon as
well as the smell of frying potatoes, which he hadn't
caught before. The others inside the saloon quickly qui-
eted down, leaving Clint to make his way to a table un-
disturbed. By the time Clint went to sit down, the noise
of his chair being pulled out squawked throughout the
entire room.

Fortunately, Clint didn't have to wait long before the
dismal atmosphere inside the place was brightened by the
reappearance of the dark-skinned woman who worked behind the bar. She emerged from the next room holding a
plate that was stacked with generous helpings of hot bacon and potatoes in each hand.

"It's not much," she said, setting the plates on the table,
"but there's plenty of it."

It wasn't exactly the most balanced meal he'd ever had,
but Clint had to admit that it smelled damn good. Just as
he picked up a fork and was about to dig, he saw the
barkeep practically jump away from the table and rush
back toward the kitchen.

"Almost forgot something," she said before disappear-
ing into the other room. When she reappeared, she was
holding a small basket covered with a rumpled white napkin. She set the basket down and flicked the napkin away
like a magician at the end of his best trick.

Clint immediately grabbed for one of the bread rolls
in the basket. Even though they were cold, he broke one
in half and took a bite. "Thanks," he said through a full
mouth.

She shrugged and cracked open a roll for herself.
"Something to sop up the grease."

"Yeah," grunted one of the nearby customers. "You'll need it."

The next roll she picked up wasn't cracked in half. Instead, she chucked the entire thing at the back of the head of the old man who'd made that last comment. The roll bounced off his skull with a louder thump than someone might normally expect from a piece of bread.

Turning back around, the barkeep was grinning widely and taking a bite out of her own roll. Clint couldn't help but be taken in by the warmth of her smile and the smooth, comfortable way she moved. Every motion was fluid and there was something catlike about her entire body.

"I'm Rebecca Barry," the barkeep said with a friendly nod.

Clint's first impulse was to respond by giving his own name. But that impulse was cut off by a reminder that came from the back of his head. "You're a fugitive," it said. "Act like one or you might as well turn yourself in."

His poker instincts helped alleviate most of the discomfort that might have shown in his eyes as he said, "My name's Adam."

He knew that if a lie was necessary, the best thing to do was keep it to a minimum. There was less to remember for the moment and less to regret later on. He only hoped that she wouldn't force him to make up a last name to go with the first.

"Hope you're hungry Adam," Rebecca said with a wink. "Like I said. There's plenty more where this came from."

THIRTY-TWO

More than once, Clint nearly forgot about the more pressing matters in his life while he was eating that simple dinner with Rebecca. He would always be brought back to reality when she would call him by the semi-fake name that he'd given her. Adam may have been close to Adams, but it referred to a man who was miles away from where he wanted to be.

Then again, sitting in a room where he got complete attention from someone as beautiful as Rebecca wasn't actually too bad.

The food, on the other hand, could have been better.

Once he'd eaten enough to take the edge off his hunger, Clint began to see why there were no other takers for a meal inside the saloon. Even the drunks knew better than to ask for a helping of greasy, leathery bacon and potatoes that had been boiled so much that they practically melted on his plate. Still, the food was a hell of a lot better than the same old slop he'd been forced to eat when camping on his own.

"So what brings you into town, Clint?" Rebecca asked while sopping up some of the juices on her plate using a hunk of bread.

"I'm headed south."

"Really? Any particular reason, or are you just trying to get someplace warmer?"

"I'm hoping to meet up with someone."

"Well, since you don't seem overly enthused about that prospect, I'm guessing you're not talking about a woman."

Clint smirked and shook his head. "No, it's not a woman."

Rebecca's smile upon hearing that was subtle, but unmistakable. "Are you staying here long then, or just passing through?"

"It looked like you had rooms to rent here, so I was hoping I might be able to take one of those off your hands for a night or two."

"There's two rooms upstairs, but they're nothing special."

"Are either of them available?"

"Yes."

"Then you've got yourself a deal."

Rebecca started to laugh and chewed on the last of her bread. "I'm a better salesman than I thought."

Clint watched the way she eyed him and had no trouble reading the signals being sent from her movements and even the position of her body. Right from the start, she'd made sure to sit close to him, and all throughout their meal, she'd brushed her knee against his and touched his arm or hand whenever half an excuse presented itself.

"I'll bet you're awfully good at plenty of things," Clint said in a voice that brought his flirtation clearly to the surface.

She caught it right away and gave him a sly, knowing smile in return. "You'd be damn right about that."

"How about you pour us something to drink and then you can show me one of those rooms?"

Pushing her chair back from the table, Rebecca

scooped up the dishes and leaned over so she could talk
to Clint without being overheard by anyone else. "Actually, I've got something much better in mind."

Clint and Rebecca did have a drink together. She'd
brewed up a fresh batch of coffee, laced it with cream,
and also added a generous splash of a smooth liquor that
Clint hadn't expected to find in some little town stuck in
the middle of nowhere. The drink sent a warm feeling that
started in their stomachs and rolled nicely through the rest
of their bodies.

While the coffee drink was fine for starters, that heat
was nothing when compared to the heat that he felt only
a few minutes after they'd drained their mugs. That was
the amount of time it took for her to lead him to a room
and push him inside as though she meant to slam him
down and take him by force.

Clint felt his shoulders bump against the wall and felt
the rumble of the door as Rebecca shoved it shut behind
her. Her eyes were wide with anticipation as she stalked
forward and licked her lips as if she was already imagining how good he was going to taste.

The clothes she wore were simple and made from a
heavy cotton designed to withstand plenty of hard work.
Rebecca pulled off her milky white blouse to reveal the
camisole that clung to her shapely body. Her dark cotton
skirt fell away from her curvy leg as she pressed herself
up against Clint and rubbed her calf up and down along
his leg and hip.

So far, Clint hadn't even had a chance to get a look at
the layout of the room he was in. He'd been carrying a
lantern, but hadn't had a chance to give the knob more
than half a turn before he'd set it down and was overtaken
by Rebecca.

After all the flirting they'd done over their drink and
all the lingering smiles and eye contact they'd had, Clint

was surprised he was able to think clearly enough to set the lantern down at all. There was an instant attraction between the two that neither one of them could deny.

Everything about her, from the dark sensuality of her gaze to the smooth brown hue of her skin, made Rebecca more and more attractive to him. As he looked at her more, he only saw more reasons to want her. Rebecca's walk was slow and sensual. Her lips were full and soft. Even the layers of her clothing couldn't keep him from noticing the proud, succulent curves of her breasts.

Her hands were strong and insistent as they moved over his body, rubbing some places while lingering in others. As she felt every inch of him she could reach, Rebecca pulled in deep, excited breaths. Her eyes were wide and almost seemed to flash in the near-darkness at him when her fingers wrapped around something to her liking.

Clint's heart raced in his chest as he felt her hand wrap firmly around his cock. Even through his pants, she rubbed him up and down, coaxing his erection until it was so hard that he ached to get it inside of her. He used that feeling to speed his own efforts to get his hands under her clothes.

The sensation of her bare skin against his hands made them both pause for a moment to savor the feeling. That pause lasted all of a second and a half before Clint hiked up her skirts with an almost desperate intensity.

"Now let's see if there's some other way I can warm you up," she whispered while lowering herself onto her knees and taking his pants down as she went.

THIRTY-THREE

Clint leaned back against the wall and ran his fingers through Rebecca's hair as her head moved between his legs. Her lips were every bit as soft as he'd imagined and when they wrapped around his cock, he felt dizzier than any amount of liquor could get him.

As she bobbed her head back and forth, Rebecca slid her tongue along his shaft. First, she licked along the bottom. Then, as she took him all the way into her mouth, she made long, lingering swirls around the head as well as down his entire length. Every so often, she would look up at him, smiling widely and letting her teeth graze ever so gently along his skin.

Soon, she closed her eyes and devoured him completely. Her head moved vigorously as she sucked him like he was a piece of candy. Her hands moved over his stomach and chest as her lips glided along his cock, clawing up over his body in a way that made him want her even more.

The instant he felt her lips move off of him, Clint reached down and pulled Rebecca back onto her feet. He didn't stop when she was upright, however. Instead, he kept on lifting her until she was completely off her feet

132

so he could turn them both around until she was the one with her back against the wall.

Clint felt one of her legs wrap around him as the other slid down his side. Even with that one leg, Rebecca was strong enough to support herself as Clint's hands moved down along her sides and then back up again to cup her firm, generous breasts.

Their bodies were pressed closely together and their hands moved freely over one another. With each one moving more out of need and instinct, Clint didn't particularly realize he'd been hiking up her skirts until they were bunched around Rebecca's waist and his penis was pushing against the warmth of her wet pussy.

Rebecca opened her legs a bit more for him and let out a pleased sigh as she felt his rigid length enter her body. A little shifting was all it took for her to adjust herself so that Clint's erection brushed against her clitoris every time it slid in and out of her.

Feeling the way her body tensed and watching the expression on her face, Clint knew real quickly that he was doing something very right and did his best to do even better. Her plump, rounded backside filled his hands as he pulled her closer and ground his hips in a circular motion with every thrust.

"Oh god," she moaned. As soon as the words were out of her mouth, Rebecca looked over to the closed door with a guilty smirk.

She and Clint could both still hear the muffled sound of voices and movement coming from the saloon's main room. There was only one other person who worked there, and he had taken over as soon as Rebecca dragged Clint away. That man's voice stopped suddenly when he'd caught a bit of Rebecca's passionate cry.

Before she could look back at Clint, Rebecca felt him moving once again inside of her. His rigid shaft teased her by pulling almost out, but then drove into her with

enough force to get her to cry out again. This time, she
was unable to form any words. All she could do was
groan with every breath as Clint glided out of her and
drove back inside.

He held on to her with both hands, massaging her
rounded buttocks while holding her in just the right position so he could push as deeply as possible between her
legs. With her arms tightening around him more and
more, Clint could feel her body starting to move in time
with his until he started groaning as well.

Clint set her down when he felt her legs loosen from
around him. The moment her feet touched the floor, Rebecca stepped away from the wall and started walking
toward the door. With one hand, she kept her skirts
bunched up around her waist to display her ample backside. With the other hand, she stroked Clint's penis while
leading him behind her.

For a moment, Clint thought she was going to head
outside again. But when she made it to the door, Rebecca
stopped and placed both hands against the frame as if she
was keeping it closed. Looking over her shoulder at him,
she arched her back and stuck her backside out in a way
that gave Clint an excellent view. When she saw him step
closer to her, she spread her legs apart a little more and
lifted her backside like an erotic offering.

Clint didn't waste a second in taking her up on that
offer. He placed one hand on her waist and used his other
to guide the tip of his cock between her thighs until it
touched the wet lips of her vagina. Rebecca's breath
caught in her throat for a second and she let it out again
only when she felt Clint bury himself all the way inside
of her.

Now, Clint could hold on to her with both hands. He
did exactly that, pulling her closer every time he thrust
his hips forward and easing her away as he pulled out.
Soon, his motions picked up and Rebecca's hands were

being slapped against the door frame. She pushed her hips out with her own rhythm, urging Clint to pound into her even harder.

In no time at all, their bodies were coming together noisily. The sound of flesh slapping against flesh filled the small room, laced with the steady grunting of both Clint and Rebecca.

Feeling her back arch when he pushed into her a certain way, Clint took hold of her firmly and entered her at the angle she liked the most. As he drove inside of her, he could feel her muscles tense and saw her head snap back with her mouth open wide.

Clint leaned forward to kiss her and she leaned back to meet him. As their lips touched, he pumped his hips forward so he could catch her cries in his own mouth. Her pussy tightened around him, massaging him to the brink of orgasm. Before the rush of pleasure started surging through him, he reached down between her legs with one hand to rub a tiny circle around her wet clitoris.

That was all he needed to do to get Rebecca's entire body twitching with anticipation and pleasure. She had to bite down on her lower lip as a powerful orgasm sent a tingling sensation throughout every inch of her flesh. Since Clint was still pumping inside of her and hitting that perfect spot, she could feel another climax hot on the heels of the first one.

This time, Clint's own pleasure was about to explode as well. His fingers tightened around Rebecca's waist, which seemed to only intensify what she was feeling at that moment. His climax built and built as he kept pumping in and out.

With the last powerful thrusts, he saw Rebecca drop her head and hold on to the wall as if that was all she could do to remain on her feet. Sweat was forming at the small of her back and running over Clint's hands in a cool trickle. With the scant bit of light in the room, the sight of that made Clint's orgasm come only that much quicker.

With one last thrust, he was sent over the edge. The pleasure he felt was so intense that his eyes seemed to rattle in his skull and his knees buckled for a moment or two. When he was finally starting to catch his breath, Clint could feel Rebecca grinding slowly against him by twitching her backside back and forth.

That motion alone got the blood pounding in Clint's ears. His orgasm dragged on for another couple of seconds before it left him almost unable to stand up himself. His grip relaxed on her hips, but his hands were reluctant to leave the smooth contours of her skin. In fact, he was doing just fine standing there in the dark, pressing against her warm body.

Suddenly, they both twitched as one. Their heads snapped up as well, responding to a noise that had broken through the muddle of their senses.

"What was that?" Rebecca asked.

Clint was already stepping back and getting his pants back up around his waist. "I'd swear it was a gunshot."

THIRTY-FOUR

Now that he'd said it out loud, Clint could still hear that gunshot in the back of his mind. There had only been one, and it had been followed by a rumble of commotion coming from the rest of the saloon. Rebecca stepped aside so she could pull her skirts down to cover herself, so Clint opened the door the moment all his buckles were fastened.

When he emerged from the narrow doorway, he was practically knocked off his feet by a familiar figure who'd been rushing down the hall in his direction. Actually, the other man hadn't been coming straight at Clint initially, but had instead been heading for the top of the stairs nearby. When he saw Clint, his eyes widened with surprise and his hand snapped upward to point his gun.

Clint's reaction was instantaneous. Coming from pure reflex, he dropped his hand down to the Colt at his side and drew the weapon before the other man could even take proper aim. Rather than take a shot, however, Clint had enough presence of mind to restrain himself. After all, killing one of the men he'd been searching for wouldn't have done him a bit of good.

With a sharp flex of his arm, Clint brought the barrel of the Colt up underneath the other man's jaw. Iron

137

cracked against bone, sending the running man straight to the floor. His arms and legs sprawled awkwardly as he hit the ground, making him look as if he was doing a strange jig on his back.

Clint put an end to that motion by stepping forward and dropping his left boot onto the other man's wrist. That pinned the guy's gun to the floor and stopped a bit of his flopping around.

"Hold still," Clint said, pushing the Colt's barrel into the other man's face.

The other man complied, his face already swelling up from where he'd been struck.

Keeping the Colt trained steadily on target, Clint glanced up at the direction from which the other man had come. One of the two doors farther down the hall was swinging slowly open and traces of black smoke still hung in the air near that spot.

"What are you doing here?" Clint asked, focusing once again on the man pinned beneath his boot.

Although the words were muffled by his bruised jaw and swollen face, the other man's message came through just fine. "Wha were you . . . oing in that gloset?"

Clint couldn't keep the smile from spreading across his face. Part of that was because of the peculiar way the other man was forced to form his words. Another part of that smile was just in appreciation of some good old-fashioned dumb luck shining in his direction.

Behind him, Rebecca poked her head out from the narrow door as well. She'd been the one to drag Clint into the small, dark room in the first place. Of course, there was no way for her to know how good of a decision that truly had been.

"What's going on out here, Adam?" Rebecca asked.

"I think it's over for now," he responded. Leering down at the other man, he asked, "Is it?"

Reluctantly, the man on his back nodded. Even that

small movement seemed to bring him a bit of pain.

Clint reached down and took a handful of the other man's shirt. Using that to haul him to his feet, Clint kept the Colt in place just to make sure to discourage any sudden moves. The pistol did its job just fine and the only movement the other fellow made was to get his feet beneath him and start walking where he was being shoved.

The three of them made an odd-looking caravan as they all moved from the hall and into the room that had the door that remained ajar. Even though the smoke had all but dissipated, the smell of gunpowder was still in the air, marking that as the definite spot where the shot had been fired.

The man with the swollen face was shoved into the room first, followed by Clint and then Rebecca. Clint took a look around and then glanced at the door. Nailed to the front of the door was a small placard with the number one painted upon it. That was the same number as the one tagged to the key Rebecca had given to him earlier.

"Shut the door," Clint said to Rebecca once everyone was inside.

After closing the door, Rebecca placed her hands on her hips and turned on both men as if she didn't know who to smack first. "What the hell is going on here?" she demanded. Turning to Clint, she asked, "And what are you still smiling about?"

"I'm just awfully glad you couldn't wait to get to a bed."

THIRTY-FIVE

Even though he'd paid to rent it for the night, Clint hadn't yet seen the inside of his room until he was there with the man who'd broken through its door. The latch was snapped off and the jamb was cracked after having been kicked in only a few minutes ago. Rebecca noticed that almost immediately, which made the frown on her face deepen.

"I'll have to have this fixed," she grumbled.

Nodding toward the bed, Clint added, "And don't forget about that, while you're at it."

Rebecca looked in that direction and saw what he'd referred to. The bed had been made with fresh linens and a blanket. Under those, there were two pillows that she'd tossed there herself in her rush to get downstairs and tend the bar.

Apparently, those pillows had looked close enough to a man's form in the darkness, because there was a blackened hole in the pillow that would have been a sleeping person's head. When she saw that, Rebecca's eyes widened and she lunged toward the bed so she could examine the damage even closer.

"You're gonna pay me back for this damage you

caused," she hollered to the man whose face was already swollen up like a ripe melon on one side.

Despite the fact that he was being held at gunpoint, the other man shifted toward Clint just to get away from Rebecca.

Clint put that man's priorities back in line by tapping the Colt's barrel against the captive's forehead. "I think this one here would like to have a seat and talk for a bit," Clint said. "If not, you can take your pick between this gun or her."

It was amusing to see that the other man still couldn't decide which of those two scared him the most. That indecision only served to settle him down faster and start him nodding vigorously to Clint's offer. Once a chair was kicked his way, the man dropped himself straight into it.

"All right then," Clint said, holstering the Colt. "Now we can talk like civilized people."

Rebecca's nostrils flared and she started to come at the other man again. "Civilized, my ass! This one here thinks he can just—" She stopped herself, however, when she saw the warning look in Clint's eye. Even she knew that she would be first in line to be hurt if the other man truly got his thoughts together and decided to make a run for it.

"You ain't the law," the other man said, suddenly finding a bit of courage. "You can't keep me here."

Clint raised his eyebrow and sat down on the edge of the bed. "Oh no? I'll tell you what. If you're so sure about that, why don't you just get up, try to walk out of here, and see what happens?"

The other man's eyes flicked between Clint's face, the Colt at his side, and the door. It didn't take long before his body slumped a bit and he resigned himself to his current situation.

"Smart man," Clint said. "Now all I want is to ask a

few questions and then we can all get on with our lives.
First of all, what's your name?"

"Jerry."

"All right, Jerry. I'm sure you know who I am."

Jerry let out an exasperated breath and nodded.

"And what's your connection to Tony Ackerman?"

"There ain't no connection no more," Jerry spat. "He's
dead. You killed him."

Although Clint wasn't looking directly at her, he could
see the way Rebecca flinched when she heard that. He
could feel her eyes on him and when he didn't say a word
to dispute the accusation, he saw her move away to stand
against a wall.

"What was your connection?"

His indignation quickly fading, Jerry lowered his eyes
and started kneading his hands. "He gave me work here
and there. Odd jobs and such."

"How odd are we talking about?"

"Just jobs. I don't know."

Clint shifted where he was sitting so he was once again
taking up a good portion of Jerry's line of sight. "You did
whatever he told you. Is that it? Is that how you and those
other two friends of yours got their money?"

"Yeah. I mean . . . no. What others?"

Clint shook his head. "No use covering up for them
now. I saw all three of you there that night. Others saw
you too. It's not like you three were experts at sneaking
around. What were you there for?"

"Just getting a breath of fresh air."

Suddenly, Clint lunged forward and pulled his arm
back as though he was about to backhand Jerry across the
sore half of his face. The other man almost fell over backwards trying to dodge the blow even though it never really
came.

"I didn't kill nobody," Jerry sputtered. "None of us
did."

"But you meant to," Clint shot back. "Or were you just out for some more fresh air tonight when you came in here blasting?"

Jerry's mouth hung open. The excuse he'd prepared obviously didn't even come close to fitting the question Clint had just asked. His mind raced to try to come up with something good enough to get him out of that room. When it didn't come, Jerry couldn't think of anything to say in its place.

"You meant to come in here and kill me," Clint stated. "If you try to deny it, I'll just have to introduce you to the holes in my bed and then give you a closer look at the damage to my door. In fact, I'll give you such a close look that you'll be picking linens and splinters out of your teeth for a month."

Jerry cringed with every one of Clint's words, but didn't look as though he was going to break. The nervousness and fear were plain to see, but there was something that kept him from snapping completely. Clint could read that well enough in the other man's eyes, which only added more fuel to his own frustration.

"What were you doing here?" Clint asked. "Tell me!"

"We saw what you did. We thought you'd be after us too."

"Why would I come after you or anyone else? Ackerman was the one calling me out."

"I don't know about all that," Jerry said. "All I know is that I saw you kill Tony and thought for sure you saw where we was hiding."

"Why were you hiding there?"

For a split second, it seemed as though the words were just going to spill out of him the way the rest had up to this point. But that little ironclad lock in Jerry's mind held yet again, keeping him from giving Clint anything else to go on.

"There's no reason to deny it," Clint pressed. "I heard

the shot. I see the bullet hole. I caught you coming out of my room. I know you meant to kill me."

Jerry straightened up and did his best to put on a brave face. "Why shouldn't I? You were the one coming after me. You tracked me down all the way here. What the hell should I do? Just sit back and wait for you to gun me down the way you did to Tony?"

Clint had plenty he could have said to that. He had plenty of questions to ask as well. The only thing holding him back from saying any of them at that moment was because he knew none of it would have done him any good. Not just then, anyway.

"Fine," Clint said, which brought a little more resolve to Jerry's face. Turning to Rebecca, Clint said, "Do me a favor, would you?"

Still rattled, she nodded and replied, "Sure. What is it?"

"Get me some rope."

That burned the resolve right out of Jerry's eyes.

THIRTY-SIX

A few minutes later, Rebecca, Clint, and Jerry were still in the same room. There was one major difference this time, however. This time, Jerry was tied up with so much rope that he looked more like an overgrown caterpillar than a man. Most of his body was wrapped in coils of rope, which made it next to impossible for him to do anything else besides wriggle slightly whenever he worked up the nerve.

Clint gave the other man a short talk on the virtues of keeping quiet and cooperating. Judging by the look in Jerry's wide eyes, there wasn't much fight left in him. At least, there wasn't nearly enough for him to work his way through those ropes.

All this time, Rebecca watched what happened and tried to stay out of the way. Once the anger over the damage done to the room had subsided, she was hit with what was behind the damage. Mainly, she couldn't seem to get her eyes off the guns worn by both Jerry and Clint.

"Sorry about what happened to the room," Clint said to Rebecca. Turning to the bed, Clint picked up a few of the things he'd taken off of Jerry before tying him up. Mainly, they were items that were too bulky or too dangerous to allow the other man to keep and consisted of a gun belt, a Bowie knife, and a money belt.

Clint took the money belt, opened it, fished out a few dollars, and left the rest. "Here," he said, offering the money to Rebecca. "This should cover it."

She took the money and nodded. "Yeah. Thanks."

Putting his arm around her, Clint led Rebecca out of the room and shut the door. Although there was no latch to keep it closed, the cracked wood fit tightly against the door so it at least wouldn't swing open. After walking down the hall toward the stairs, Clint stopped and looked directly into Rebecca's eyes.

"Are you all right?" he asked.

She laughed once and shook her head. "Oh sure. This happens every day around here. Can't you tell?"

"Would it make you feel better to go in there and smack him around a little? In fact, work on the other side of his face. At least that should balance him out."

Rebecca knew Clint was joking and even though it looked like she didn't want to laugh, she couldn't hold it back very long. She was glad for that because once she allowed herself a laugh or two, she felt her shoulders finally drop from where they'd been pulled up under her ears. When she looked back up at him, her smile only remained for a second before it was replaced by the concerned frown that had been there before.

Without a word, Rebecca took hold of Clint's arm and started dragging him toward the stairs. A small group was gathered down there, consisting mainly of the old men who'd been drinking in the saloon.

"Need any help up there?" one of the old men asked.

Rebecca looked first at Clint and then down to her customers. "No, it's fine."

"We heard a scuffle up there. And was that a gunshot?"

"No, no. Just a little misunderstanding is all. Someone thought this one here was sleeping with another man's wife," she explained, hooking a thumb toward Clint.

Clint could hear the tension in Rebecca's voice, but apparently her explanation was good enough for everyone else. After a few more assurances from Rebecca, the others downstairs started swapping unfaithful wife stories of their own and eventually wandered back to their drinks.

Still holding Clint's elbow, Rebecca pulled him past the stairs, looked around in exasperation, and finally led him back into the closet. After all the commotion, the closet seemed even smaller and more cramped than it had before. Of course, the last time they'd been in there, the close quarters weren't a problem. This time, the occasion wasn't quite as friendly.

"What's going on here?" Rebecca asked. "First I think I'm just passing the night with a good man and then I hear shots going off and hear talk of murder."

"I'm sorry about all of that, Rebecca. You've got to believe that I didn't want you to get wrapped up in all of this."

"But you said you were looking for someone. If you knew he was here, then how could I not get wrapped up in it with you spending so much time with me?"

"I knew he was in town. I didn't know he was right here in this building. Besides, I've been tracking this man and his friends for a little bit and so far they've done their best to steer clear of me."

"Yeah," Rebecca said with a short laugh. "I can certainly see why they'd do that."

Rather than try to answer her right away, Clint held his tongue and took her in both arms. Rebecca struggled at first, but a little gentle insistence was all it took to get her to relax. Clint could feel the change in her as if some harder shell had melted away to leave the soft, warm body he'd become so intimately familiar with.

Eventually, her arms slid around his waist and she let out a deep breath. When she was feeling better again,

Rebecca pushed back enough so she could look straight into Clint's face.

"What are you going to do with him?" she asked.

"I plan on taking him to the law, but just not yet."

"Why wait? Are you after a bounty?"

"No," Clint replied. "I'm after the other two that were riding with him. If I turn this one in to the law, it won't solve a thing. I have a feeling once I get all three of them together and they see there's no other way out, they'll become a little more cooperative."

Her eyes dropped down for a second before she asked, "Is it true? What he said you did. Is that true?"

"Yeah," Clint admitted. "It is. I did kill a man, but he left me no choice. I'm after these others because they know what really happened and can clear it up in the eyes of the law."

"But . . . why would they?"

Clint felt as though a cold rock had just been dropped into his stomach. That was a real good question. Unfortunately, Clint wasn't sure he could answer it.

THIRTY-SEVEN

Rebecca made a brief appearance downstairs behind the bar, but she found a reason to excuse herself pretty quickly. Clint spent some time down there as well, but wasn't as concerned with keeping up appearances. He had a beer to steady his nerves and took some time to listen to what others were saying about what had happened.

The locals were guarded around him to be sure, but once they saw how comfortable Rebecca was around him, Clint didn't feel so much like an outsider. Most of the talk was in regards to matters that had nothing to do with much of anything. There was bragging about fights and sexual conquests and even a few dirty jokes, but nothing for Clint to be too worried about.

As far as anyone there was concerned, the scuffle was just that: just a simple scuffle, the likes of which happened fairly regularly when folks got together with liquor in their systems. Before too long, Clint said his good-byes to Rebecca and left the saloon. He walked out into the cold air, got himself acclimated to the chill, and then started walking.

Arrowhead Creek was a quiet enough place. More importantly, it was small enough that sound was carried

much easier than when bigger quantities of larger buildings were involved. For a town the size of the one Clint
was in at the moment, wind mostly traveled as though it
was rolling over open land. Apart from making the cold
rip through him like a knife, it made it that much easier
for Clint to figure out if he was being followed.

Even without snow on the ground, boots tended to
crunch louder when the dirt beneath them was cold. Ice
cracked like bits of glass and heavier clothes rustled that
much louder as a person moved within them. Keeping a
casual expression on his face, Clint walked down the
street while his ears stretched out to pick up anything of
interest.

After all the work he'd done and all the efforts he'd
put into tracking down those three men, Clint found himself hoping to be ambushed. At least that way he could
see his targets close-up and would get a chance to bring
them in once and for all.

But the question still remained as to what would happen when he did get ahold of them. Rebecca had a point.
Why would they help him? Whenever Clint had thought
of that before, he'd put off answering it until he at least
got hold of one or two of the men he was after. Well, he
had one man, but the answer to that question still hung
out of his reach.

It would have been easier if Clint was the sort to use
the more darker methods of persuasion. While not above
putting the fear of God into a man for the proper reason,
Clint wasn't about to follow through on his more colorful
threats. Once he started down that road, he knew only too
well that crossing the line would just become easier every
time after that. The whole reason for his jailbreak and
subsequent manhunt was to make good on the line that
had been crossed against him. His only hope in coming
out of this intact would be to make sure he showed the

right people who'd really crossed that line, without stepping over it too much himself.

It was a difficult business, to be sure. Now more than ever, Clint saw the appeal of just tossing the law completely and doing whatever the hell he wanted. It would be a hell of a lot easier and he could do whatever the hell he wanted.

The only thing was that men didn't live that way.

Animals did.

With that thought in mind, Clint found himself standing in precisely the same spot in which he'd started. He was still a fugitive from the law and he still didn't know exactly how to fix it. All that left for him to do was try to keep out of the fire for as long as possible while trying to come up with a real plan to clear his name in the process.

Clint liked to think of himself as an optimist. Times like these, however, made him feel like anything but.

Without breaking his stride, Clint rounded a corner and started looking at what was waiting for him on the next street. He picked out something that suited his needs perfectly and rushed for it as soon as the right moment presented itself.

Having spotted a recessed doorway on a building at the corner, Clint jogged up to the doorway and pressed his back up against the wall. Now concealed completely in shadow, he held his breath just to make sure that the trail of steam wouldn't give his position away.

He waited there for a moment, still certain that he heard some slight sound behind him moments before he'd rounded that corner. Replaying the sound again and again in his mind, he became certain that there had been someone behind him.

That certainty faded, however, as seconds turned into a minute and that minute turned into a few minutes. But still he waited there in the darkness with his hand over the grip of his Colt, waiting to get a look at another of those three men he was after.

Just as he was starting to doubt his own senses, Clint heard a set of footsteps crunching in the snow. They were quiet and steady, making their way around the corner as though looking for something that they were afraid might just get away from them.

A sly grin crossed Clint's face as he spotted the shadows and then the figures of two people round the corner and head straight for him.

Both figures revealed themselves to him since they seemed completely oblivious to the fact that Clint was even there. They weren't even looking in his direction. Instead, they were gazing up at the stars and pointing toward them while whispering to one another.

It wasn't the two Clint had been hoping to find. Instead, it was merely a couple out for a stroll. The woman was tall, which put her at about the same height as her escort. Her arm was entwined with his and she nodded while he told her some secret or another about the part of the heavens he was pointing toward.

Clint felt like a fool. He would have felt even more foolish if he'd been spotted standing there like a monster lurking in the shadows. Whether it was because of Clint's skill at remaining hidden or the fact that the couple was more interested in the stars didn't matter. What mattered was that they kept right on walking until they were far enough away for Clint to step out safely.

Even with his mistake still fresh in his mind, he couldn't shake the feeling that the men he was after were close. He looked around carefully and took in every sight as well as every sound. All he got was the picture of stillness that was the darkened street and the cold rustle of the wind swirling past his ears.

As a last-ditch effort, Clint stepped even farther away from the building until he was standing in the middle of the street. He walked slowly back toward the Double Barrel Saloon without even trying to quiet his steps.

He made it all the way back without catching more than a chill from the wintry night's cold.

Even though he'd been wrong about being followed, Clint knew better than to doubt his instincts about much else. The other two were close. He would have staked his life on it. They might not have been breathing down his neck or even aware that Clint was in Arrowhead Creek, but those other two were still close.

Either that, or Clint was close to finding where those others were. Just thinking that got his heart beating faster, and he knew he'd just hit the proverbial nail on the head.

After what felt like months on the run, Clint was finally closing in on what he'd been chasing after.

He was so close.

If nothing else, Clint was certain of that.

THIRTY-EIGHT

"I'll need the key to that other room," Clint said once he caught Rebecca at a quiet moment.

She turned to him and paused. That little pause was enough to tell Clint a whole lot. She might have done a good job of hiding her fear, but it wasn't good enough to convince someone who just plain knew better.

"There's a jail cell in the sheriff's office," she replied. "So far, nobody called him over here, but that's just because nobody knows there's any reason to."

"Actually," Clint added, lowering his voice a bit more, "that's the way I'd like to keep it."

"What? Why?"

"It's a long story, but I can assure you that the law's going to find out about the whole thing. They just need to wait until I have all the pieces. Otherwise, it won't turn out too good."

"Not too good for you, you mean?"

"Yeah."

A hopeful smile started to form on her face. "Because you didn't kill that man like that fella upstairs said you did, right?"

Clint winced at that. More than anything, he wanted to

lie to her. Even though he'd only known her a short amount of time, it rubbed Clint the wrong way to have someone regard him like that. Killing another human being was never easy. Having that combined with being looked at like a murderous animal just made it all worse.

"Right?" Rebecca asked again.

"No. I killed him."

Some of the hope that had been in her eyes faded away like the light from a candle that had been snuffed. "Was it like you said? Was the other one the one who started it?"

The saloon had cleared out for the most part, leaving only a couple of the old-timers slouched over their drinks. Clint took Rebecca by the hand and pulled her away from the bar.

"Come on," he said. "I'll tell you everything that happened."

The story didn't take long.

Rebecca listened without interrupting him once, nodding every so often as a way to let him know that she was paying attention. But Clint didn't even need those nods. He could tell by the intensity in her eyes that she was doing her level best to soak up every last word.

He knew he didn't have to explain everything to her. After all, he'd only known the woman for a matter of hours. When he laid it all out for her, he did so as a way to straighten it all out in his own mind as well. Stepping back for a minute or two and getting a good look at everything that had come before was a way for him to make sure he was truly in the right.

All this time, there had been that lingering doubt whether or not he'd done the right thing. The funny thing was that shooting Ackerman was the most serious act he'd committed, but doing it had been the easiest choice to make. There was no doubt about that one. His life was in danger, as was Emma's. Tony Ackerman had forfeited his own life in Clint's eyes.

The tricky part was in him breaking out of jail and running from the law. No matter how many times he'd justified it in his mind, Clint still felt uncomfortable about all of that. Part of him wondered if he could truly return to a normal life after walking out of that jail cell of his own accord.

Another part of him wondered if he even deserved a normal life.

Rebecca sat back in her chair and nodded slowly once Clint was finished speaking. They were sitting at a table in the back of the saloon where the crackle of the fireplace was loud enough to drown out the hushed whisper of Clint's tale.

"I need a drink," she said, getting up and turning toward the bar. "How about you?"

"Just coffee, thanks."

She went and got the drinks. In front of Clint, she set down a mug of warm coffee and she took a shot of whiskey for herself. When she raised the drink to her lips, Rebecca paused and let the smell of the liquor drift into her senses before taking a sip that was just big enough for her to feel the burn as it trickled down her throat.

"You want to know what I think?" she asked.

"Yes, I would."

"I think you're lucky to be alive."

Oddly enough, Clint hadn't been expecting to hear anything close to that.

"You look surprised."

"And you look like an excellent judge of character."

"Well, it sounds to me like that judge was set to hang you before he even laid eyes on you. And as for the marshal, it seems like he was either too lazy or too weak to do anything else but go along with the judge. That is," she added, looking into Clint's eyes, "if what you told me was true."

Rather than jump to his own defense, Clint held her gaze until she looked down at her drink again.

After another sip, Rebecca said, "And I think it's true. Every word of it. Someone would have to be blind not to think that, especially since you weren't the one to shoot up my place and since that asshole upstairs sure as hell ain't no deputy."

Clint chuckled partly at the way Rebecca said that last part, but mostly because it felt so good to have someone else on his side.

"There's just one thing, though," she added. "I can't have a wanted man staying with me. I'll help you because it sounds like you need it, but I can't have you stay here, Clint. I'm sorry."

"Don't be sorry," he said, patting her hand. "You don't have anything to apologize for. I should be apologizing to you for getting you into this."

"Glad you understand. Now just wait here for a bit and I'll take you someplace you can get a good night's sleep."

"But I thought you said—"

"I said I couldn't have you here. By that I mean this saloon. I sure as hell ain't going to leave you in the cold."

"Thank you" was all Clint could say.

Yes, indeed. It sure felt good to have someone else on his side.

THIRTY-NINE

Clint had been expecting to be offered a room in a cabin somewhere or possibly even a night in Rebecca's home. What he got was something entirely different. Unlike most other surprises he'd been getting as of late, this one was more than welcome.

The house Clint was taken to was one of the biggest in town. Actually, it was just outside of town, but the property seemed to extend into the limits of Arrowhead Creek. In fact, going by the twinkle of pale moonlight upon sheets of rough ice, the property encompassed a good portion of that creek itself.

"Where are you taking me?" Clint asked.

Rebecca was riding a chestnut brown mare right next to Eclipse. Flashing him her smile, she replied, "Funny for you to only get around to asking that now. Are you in the habit of blindly following strange women? Perhaps that's why you get into so much trouble."

"You know something? You might have a real good point there."

They rode up to the house, which just seemed to get bigger the closer they got. Clint recognized the spread since he'd spotted it on his way into town when he'd first arrived. Even then, however, he didn't know it was all one place and not a collection of smaller homes or possibly even a barn.

She took him to the stables, which were some of the best he'd seen in some time. The building itself was well maintained and clean as a stable could be. Parts of the structure even looked new despite the large collection of animals inside.

"There's a stall or two over there for your horse," Rebecca said. "Pick whichever one you want."

Actually, Clint didn't have to pick. Eclipse took the lead on that account by heading straight for the first empty batch of straw he could see. "Is all of this yours?" Clint asked, climbing down from the saddle so he could open the gate to the stall.

"It belongs to my family. My parents are gone, but my auntie and uncle took me in when I was young."

"Has your family always been wealthy?"

"Only over the last ten years or so. My uncle won a ranch in a game of faro and he worked it all the way up into something special."

"I'll say. Special doesn't even seem to do it justice. I wouldn't mind meeting your uncle. He sounds like a character."

"He is. I know he'd get a kick out of meeting you as well, but he and my auntie are away for the next week or so. They went into Cheyenne for supplies and such."

"I see."

They both let that statement lay right where it was. Considering how they'd spent a good portion of their time alone together, it seemed fairly obvious to both of them where their thoughts were headed. No matter what else was going on at the time, Clint and Rebecca would still glance over at each other with the familiarity that only lovers could share.

A lot had happened since the last time they'd kissed,

however. It hadn't been that long ago, but plenty had
changed. For one thing, they weren't even truly alone in
that stable. Without considering their four-legged companions, there was still one other who was along for the
ride.

After taking the saddle off of Eclipse's back, Clint
drew his knife from its scabbard and moved toward the
bundle that was tied behind the saddle to Eclipse's loin
and hind quarters. Since Jerry's arms and legs were tightly
bound, Clint had figured that the other man wouldn't be
too eager to squirm off of the Darley Arabian's back.

He was right. Throughout the entire ride, not only had
Jerry kept perfectly still, but he'd been too petrified to say
a word. The only thing securing him to the stallion was
a loop of rope connecting him to the back of the saddle.
Now that that was cut and the saddle was gone, it was up
to Jerry's own balance to keep him from falling.

"Wh . . . what are you doin'?" Jerry stammered. Just
turning his head to look at Clint as he asked that question
was enough to blow the delicate balance he'd stricken. Of
course, Eclipse being eager to shed the extra weight off
his lower back didn't help matters.

With a worried groan from the back of his throat, Jerry
slid right off of Eclipse and landed in a heap on the straw-
covered floor.

"Thanks for catching me," Jerry said sarcastically.

Clint looked down at him and winked. "Thanks for
trying to kill me."

Finished with putting her own horse up for the night,
Rebecca stepped up behind Clint and said, "Come on. I'll
show you the main house."

Jerry's eyes widened. "You're just gonna leave me out
here? I'll freeze! I'll be trampled if these gates come
loose!"

"You'll shut the hell up is what you'll do," Clint said.
With that, he scooped up Jerry and slung him over his
shoulder.

FORTY

As much as Clint would have liked to spend some time that night alone with Rebecca, there simply wasn't any time for him to spare. She took him on a quick tour of the grounds, which pretty much consisted of what they could see during their walk from the stables to the main house. As impressive as the spread had been from a distance, it was even more so up close.

Clint couldn't help but wonder just how high the stakes at that faro game had been or who the original owner of the place was. That was either one hell of a wager, or the loser of that bet was so filthy rich that he could afford to put a place like that on the table. Those possibilities passed through Clint's mind as he was taken to the main house, but didn't stay there too long.

He had bigger fish to fry at the moment, and the first item on his list was holing up someplace safe for the night. Since it seemed as though he, Rebecca, and Jerry were the only people on the entire spread, that place was as safe as Clint could get while still keeping a roof over his head. There were several caves or holes in the ground that might have been safer, but once Clint was shown to the bedroom Rebecca assigned him for the night, camping out simply wouldn't have sufficed.

"You sure he'll be alright in there?" Rebecca asked, nodding toward the smaller room connected to the bedroom.

"I already double-checked his ropes and made so many knots around him that this whole house would have to come down before he got away." When he saw the uncertainty on her face, Clint added, "And I was just about to check him again."

He went into the room, which was only slightly smaller than a few hotel rooms he'd rented over the years. Technically speaking, the room was a closet, but there were only a few suits of clothes hanging from one of the racks.

Jerry lay in a bundle like an inchworm. He was too tired to squirm any longer, so he'd simply reverted to staying put and keeping his mouth shut. Clint squatted down to check the knots he'd made. A built-in shoe rack ran along the back wall of the closet and since there were only a couple pairs of boots on the rack, the rest of the sturdy structure was open. The rope looped around the thick wooden slats no fewer than seven times along the length of Jerry's body. Not one of those loops gave more than a fraction of an inch when Clint tugged on them.

"He's not going anywhere," Clint said, straightening up and turning back to Rebecca.

Comforted by his thorough check of the prisoner's bonds, she stepped up to him and rubbed her hands over Clint's chest. "And neither are you. You're about to fall over, Clint, and don't try to tell me any different."

"I could use some shut-eye, that's for sure."

"So lay down here," she said, pulling him toward a huge bed covered by a feather mattress and down comforter, "and take all the rest you need. I'll even fetch you some fresh blankets if you like."

The moment Clint's back hit the bed, he could feel his

eyelids becoming heavier than lead. "Don't bother," he said in a groggy voice. "This'll do just fine."

He just barely managed to get the words out before he felt himself drifting off to sleep. Just before unconsciousness took him over completely, he felt the warm weight of Rebecca's body settling down next to him. Her arm draped over his body and her head rested upon his shoulder.

After that, Clint was too far gone to remember anything else.

Clint awoke the next morning to a loud, abrupt thump. Before his eyes were even open all the way, he was sitting bolt upright with his hand closed around the grip of his Colt. Before he could clear leather, he spotted the source of the noise that had pulled him from his sleep.

Standing in place like a statue caught in an awkward pose, Rebecca was still wincing in the doorway to Clint's room. She was dressed in a fresh change of clothes and was carrying a tray stacked with various bits of food. "Sorry about that," she said when Clint looked at her. "I dropped your silverware."

Although he could tell he wasn't in any danger, Clint was still too groggy to tell much else. "What time is it?"

"Just past seven. I wanted to let you sleep for a while, but I thought you both might be hungry."

Clint glanced toward the closet door, which was still wide open. Inside, he could see the shape of Jerry still wrapped up and laying right where he'd been left the night before. Sunlight streamed into the room, casting a wide ray onto the tightly bound prisoner.

Despite the fact that he could have gladly taken a few more hours of sleep, Clint felt much better after stretching his arms and working some of the kinks from his neck and back. "What've you got there?" he asked, nodding toward the tray in Rebecca's hands.

"Just whatever I could find around here. Without my auntie to cook, I eat most of my meals at the Double Barrel, so there isn't much. Just some bread and jam as well as some strips of jerked venison. I made some coffee too. There's enough for all of us." She added that last part hesitantly, looking at Clint as though she wasn't sure just how well he was going to treat the man cinched up in the closet.

"I'll be sure he gets something to eat." Having seen Jerry open his eyes and squirm a bit, Clint looked toward the closet and said, "He needs all his strength so he can help me track down his two friends. Isn't that right, Jerry?"

Even though his face had swollen up a bit more overnight, Jerry managed to spit some words out. "Go vuck yourselv."

Clint walked up to Rebecca, took the tray from her hands, and planted a long, passionate kiss on her lips. By the time he was done, he could feel her body leaning against him for support.

"What was that for?" she asked breathlessly, once the kiss was done.

"To thank you," Clint replied. "For everything."

"Just promise me you won't do anything to make this worse."

"Trust me, if I was going to kill anyone else, I would have done it already. Things would have been a whole lot easier if a man in my position would have just blasted out of jail and kept riding. I'm not that sort and I think you know that."

Rebecca nodded, running her hands up and down along Clint's sides. "I do. There's just something about you that makes it easy for me to believe you. I guess it's kind of a gut instinct. You know what I mean?"

"Yeah. I certainly do."

Clint turned toward the spot where he'd set the tray

down and picked it up again. Even though the rolls were stale and the jerked venison could have been a week old, the food looked awfully good. The coffee was strong enough so that even just the smell of it was enough to wake him up.

"All right, Jerry," Clint said while heading into the closet. "Time to eat."

Breakfast was quick. Afterward, Clint took Jerry with him to the stables and allowed him to stretch his legs while Eclipse was saddled and prepared for the day's ride. The prisoner was too exhausted to make any escape attempt but was tied back up again just as he started to regain all the feeling in his arms and legs.

Rebecca gave Clint the rest of the food she could find that would be suitable for a ride, which included canteens of water, coffee, the remaining jerky, and some dry rations.

"Come back to see me when this is over," she said. "I really want to know how this turns out."

"Me too," Clint said. And with that, he rode away from the spread with Jerry tied securely to Eclipse's back.

FORTY-ONE

It was amazing how a long ride spent flopping on the back of a horse could loosen a reluctant man's tongue. Judging by the pained look on Jerry's face, that ride had loosened a hell of a lot more than just his tongue. By the time Clint brought the Darley Arabian to a stop alongside an open stretch of trail, he heard the bound man screaming for attention.

Jerry had been hollering about one thing or another, but Clint had pretty much ignored all of it. Most of the rants started out as threats and quickly became pleas to be untied. He'd complained of everything from numbness to broken ribs, none of which garnered so much as a backwards glance from Clint.

Since he knew he wasn't causing Jerry much more than some serious discomfort, Clint hadn't had any trouble blocking out the other man's shouts. Three words caught his attention right away, however. They were the three words Clint had been waiting for the entire day.

"I'll tell you," Jerry whined. When he felt the stallion shift beneath him as though it was about to lurch into a trot once again, Jerry repeated himself at the top of his lungs. "I'll tell you!"

Clint twisted around as if it was the first time he'd noticed the extra load he'd been carrying. "What was that?"

"I said I'll tell you! I'll tell you whatever you want to know, just for the love of God, get me offa here!"

Swinging down from the saddle, Clint took his time walking around Eclipse until he could look straight into Jerry's eyes. "Having a bit of a change of heart?"

"Yeah, yeah, just untie these vucking robes."

The swelling in the prisoner's face had gone down a bit, but his words still slurred slightly when he tried to put too much emphasis in them. Spit was frozen to his chin as were the tears that had streamed down his cheeks throughout the course of the bumpy ride.

Clint put on a dissatisfied scowl. "That's not a very polite way to ask a favor, Jerry."

After a long, tired sigh, the prisoner gritted his teeth and said, "Please. Please untie these goddamn robes!"

As funny as it was to listen to Jerry's speech shift from good to bad, Clint took out his blade and severed enough of the ropes to allow Jerry to slide off of Eclipse's back. This time, he made sure to catch him before Jerry dropped onto the cold ground.

"There," Clint said after lowering Jerry to a sitting position. "See how much better things work out for you when you're polite?"

The prisoner sucked in a breath as though he meant to spit out another garbled curse, but thought better of it at the last moment. Rather than say what he was thinking, Jerry merely nodded and shifted on the ground.

"Now what was it you wanted to tell me?" Clint asked.

"Virst, I want you to promise to let me go."

"Let you go? Why would I do that?"

"If I help you."

"If you help me, I'll let you live. How's that sound?"

A frown formed on Jerry's face that was so deep, it

seemed as though his head had just cracked apart into a
thick black line. "You won't kill me. You would've done
it already."

"You've seen me kill," Clint said, looking Jerry
straight in the eyes. "Are you sure you don't think I'll
hesitate before I put some worm like you out of your
misery?"

Jerry looked into Clint's eyes and felt a chill run
through his body which had nothing to do with the wintry
breeze. All the courage he'd been building up while
bouncing on Eclipse's back in his inchworm bundle suddenly flew away like so much steam.

When he saw Jerry look away, Clint knew the other
man had bought the threat hook, line, and sinker. Of
course he wasn't about to murder anyone. Of course what
he'd told Jerry had been a bluff. Being able to pull off
bluffs that size were what separated small-time poker
players from the ones who belonged at the high-stakes
tables.

"You're the one who started this conversation," Clint
reminded him. "So why don't you just tell me what you
wanted to tell me?"

"I was supposed to meet them," Jerry admitted reluctantly.

"All right," Clint urged, once he could tell the words
weren't exactly going to flow from the other man's
mouth. "Go on."

"We all agreed on a place to go if things went bad.
We done some jobs together before and we had this place
picked out just in case we had to scatter."

"And why'd you have to scatter this time?"

Jerry looked up at him like he was surprised that question had even been asked. "Because you're Clint Adams.
You're The Gunsmith. After the way things went down
with Tony, and since we knew you seen us, we figured
we'd best get out of there before you gunned us down."

"Did Kyle tell you all that?"

"Yes, he—" Stopping himself, Jerry winced at his slip of the tongue.

"I know about Kyle, so you might as well tell me who the other one is."

"Stewart Jenna. That's the third one's name."

"And the name of the meeting place?"

After another couple of seconds to think it over, Jerry finally spit it out. "It's a little town called Memento just southeast of here. Maybe another day's ride."

"So what were you three doing there that night when Ackerman called me out?" Clint asked.

"I said enough already," Jerry answered through a sudden trembling that had overtaken his mouth.

"Then maybe you can answer something else for me."

"What?"

"How come you were in Arrowhead Creek when you should have been meeting up with your friends in Memento?"

"I . . . I thought you'd be after us and would kill every one of us when you got there."

"So you left your friends high and dry just to avoid meeting up with me? I believe that's what you might call poetic justice."

FORTY-TWO

Kyle Evans wasn't a very big man. That wasn't because of his stature, because he was actually an inch or so taller than most. What made him seem smaller was the way his back was hunched over and the way he tended to keep to the shadows or close to a wall whenever possible. It was the weight of his sins bearing down on him like lead bars hanging from his neck that shrank him down.

Kyle Evans was a hunted man and he knew it. That was enough weight to crush anyone.

"Where the hell is he?" Kyle snarled.

He turned his face toward the other man sitting next to him. It was a face that was sunken in after several days of quick meals consisting of only a bite or two of food and coated with dirt after riding hard and sleeping on the ground. Even though he'd spent the last couple of days in town, neither he nor his companion were willing to show their faces in a hotel or anyplace else where they might be easily spotted.

The man next to Kyle looked equally haggard, but was lacking the fire that was still burning in Kyle's eyes. He was a bigger man than Kyle, but had the appearance of a once bulky rock that had been worn down after sitting too long under a waterfall. He was beyond the point of looking dangerous and desperate. Stewart Jenna just looked tired and scared.

"How the hell should I know where he's at?" Stewart replied. "He knew just like I did to come here." Suddenly, his breath stopped and he fixed wide eyes upon Kyle. "Maybe he's dead."

"Don't talk that way."

"Why the hell not? We scattered because of Adams, so maybe Adams caught up to Jerry and gunned him down!"

Kyle's hand snapped out to grab Stewart by the front of his shirt. He pulled him closer so his fierce whispers could be heard. "You want to get us both killed? Then just keep right on blabbing like that so everybody looks at us funny."

The truth of the matter was that plenty of folks were already looking at them with wary suspicion. The pair had been in town a few days and had poked their heads out enough for the locals to take notice. So far, Kyle and Stewart had been keeping to themselves, but when one of them got overly anxious, it definitely caused ripples in the pond.

At the moment, the men were sitting in the back of a little shop run by an Oriental family. The shop catered to more exotic cravings and the owners knew better than to pry into the affairs of their customers. The old Chinese man was no outlaw, but didn't mind taking their money if they wanted to buy things ranging from opium to a woman for the night.

Colorful paintings hung on the walls, stained by smoke and old age. The old man and his wife shuffled about quietly, not wanting to disturb their customers' drug-induced oblivion. The old man's eyes were still sharp and his ears were even sharper. He knew the pair in the back could be trouble, so he kept them quiet his own way and made sure not to provoke them.

"You think he'll say anything to anyone?" Stewart asked, shooting a glance toward the old Chinaman.

After a moment, Kyle shook his head slowly and released his grip on Stewart. "Nah. He don't care. We're paying him plenty and that's enough for him. But if you keep going on like that, you'll call down more thunder than we can handle, so just sit tight and keep quiet. You hear me?"

"Yeah, yeah. I hear ya. But what if Jerry don't show?"

"We'll give him until noon. After that . . ." He trailed off and rubbed the heels of his hands into his eyes. "What time is it, anyway?"

Stewart started to say something, but then took it back. Instead, he struggled to his feet and staggered toward the flap of thick canvas that hung down to cover the front entrance to the shop. When the sunlight hit his eyes in full force, it temporarily blinded him. The inside of the shop was always kept in soothing shadow, making it tough to keep track of the hours.

Stewart pulled the flap back down and it still took him a few moments to clear the red haze from his vision. His head actually hurt from the sunlight, which made him wonder just how long he and Kyle had been hiding in the dark.

"It might be past noon already," Stewart said when he finally made his way back to where his partner was waiting.

The Chinese man leaned toward them and said, "It's past one thirty in afternoon."

Kyle rewarded the old man with a nasty look and didn't take his eyes away until the Chinaman bowed once and left him alone. "All right then," Kyle said to Stewart. "We'll make it midnight then. We've been waiting here long enough and if he doesn't show by then, we'll move on without him."

"I don't want to stay here that long," Stewart said. Opening his eyes all the way, he lowered himself down onto a large, embroidered pillow. "If we got CI—" He was cut off in midsentence by a warning glare from Kyle. "If we were tracked here," Stewart continued in a more cautious tone, "then we should get moving now. We shouldn't have waited here this long. Do you even know how long we've been here?"

"Of course I do. That's why I'm only giving him until midnight."

Although he didn't look too happy about it, Stewart knew that arguing about things wasn't going to make them any better. In fact, he could feel his nerves starting to pull tighter like straps of worn leather that were about to snap inside of him.

Kyle felt that same tension as well and tried to relieve it by pulling in a deep breath of the smoky air and letting it out. It wasn't quite enough to make him feel better, so he snapped his fingers at the Chinaman.

"I know what we need," Kyle said.

Stewart shook his head instantly. "No more of that stuff."

"Come on. How about some of that absinthe?"

Before Stewart could reply, he heard the rustle of heavy material followed by the blinding light of the sun flooding into the shop. The Chinaman, his wife, and a few of the customers glanced over with a bit of a wince, but the two men in the back shielded their eyes like vampires.

"I can help you?" the Chinaman's wife asked while walking toward the figure in the doorway.

"Yeah," Clint said. "I'm here to visit those two in the back. You might want to clear everyone else out of here."

FORTY-THREE

The Chinese woman took one look at the seriousness in Clint's eyes and immediately signaled to her husband. Between the two of them, the elderly couple rounded up the few other customers and herded them past Clint through the front door.

That left the shop empty except for Clint and the two men he'd been tracking. Despite the fact that there were still those three people inside the shop, the dark, smoky space felt like a tomb. For the next couple of moments, the only thing moving was the smoke in the air. The only sound to be heard was the rustle of wind on the other side of the walls.

So far, Kyle and Stewart hadn't moved a muscle. They'd watched as the place was cleared out and still watched now that only Clint was there to stare right back at them. Not that they hadn't wanted to do something. Their minds were spurring them to draw or throw something or do anything at all.

But no matter how much their minds screamed, their bodies remained rooted in place. Clint's eyes kept them there until Clint decided to break the silence himself.

"Well, well, well," Clint said, savoring the moment as

174

well as the startled expressions on the other two men's faces. "I've been looking all over for you fellas."

There was another moment of silence where neither Kyle nor Stewart knew quite what they should do. Once their initial shock wore off, however, each one glanced over to the other and they regained their ability to heed the panicked orders coming from inside their heads.

Clint could see the transformation taking place within the other two men. In fact, he'd counted on that very thing when he came barging straight in through the front door. After what he'd learned from Jerry, it was easy enough to tell that he wasn't dealing with cold-blooded killers. They may have been dangerous men, but that was still a far cry from professional shootists.

All that remained now was to put his theory to the test, and Clint meant to do just that. By the looks of things, it was going to be a trial by fire.

The first one to make a move for his gun was Stewart. The fear that had been building inside of him boiled over in the space of a second, causing his hand to snap straight to the gun hanging at his hip. Seeing that bit of motion from the corner of his eye, Kyle was the next to move toward arming himself.

After sitting in one spot for so long, feeling the desperation build to a head, finally clearing leather felt like a blessing. Even though this was exactly what Clint had been dreading, at least it was finally happening and would probably be over soon.

Clint stood like a statue in front of the other two, looking on as the storm he'd created roiled before him. The other two got their fingers on their pistols before him, but they were still doing exactly what Clint had been hoping for.

They were panicking and they were rushing. In any kind of fight, neither of those things was any good whatsoever.

Waiting until the last possible moment, Clint launched himself into motion like an arrow that had been loosed from its bow. First he ducked low and then bent his left knee so his entire body tilted to that side. He then pushed off with his right leg while the hand on that side flashed down to draw the modified Colt from its resting place.

Stewart and Kyle took their shots within half a second of each other. Just as Clint had figured, both men's shots were rushed and neither one of them came anywhere close to hitting anything except for the walls or ceiling. Both shots roared inside the enclosed space, filling the shop like the voice of one of the many dragons painted on the posts or trim.

Clint was already sailing to the left and bringing his Colt up to aim at the closest available target. Pointing the gun as though it was an extension of his own hand, Clint squeezed his trigger and sent a piece of hot lead whipping through the air. The bullet sped across the room, burrowed through a thin layer of flesh and kept right on going until it planted itself in a wall behind Stewart.

Stewart's eyes widened and his mouth gaped open, but he didn't make a sound. The pain coursing through him had stolen the breath from his lungs as it burned throughout the entire bottom half of his body. As his weight shifted, the pain exploded to an even higher plane until the entire world tilted crazily around him.

As Stewart crumpled over and fell down, his voice was still choking in the back of his throat. Kyle looked over to see what had happened and his eyes went immediately to the bloodstain spreading across Stewart's leg. The dark crimson stain was centered on Stewart's knee and spread visibly even in the split second that Kyle watched.

By this time, Clint had hit the floor on his side and was already twisting himself around so he could wind up on his belly. From there, he sighted down the Colt's barrel and waited for the space of a heartbeat.

Normally, that wasn't a whole lot of time.

When the lead was flying, however, that was enough time to decide a man's fate.

One thing was for certain: it was enough time for Kyle Evans to make one of the biggest mistakes of his life. Now that he could focus on where Clint had landed, Kyle gritted his teeth and swung his gun around to aim at that spot of the floor.

Clint saw it happening as if Kyle's twitching trigger finger was the only thing moving in the room. His eyes focused on that spot as his reflexes kicked in to answer the shot before it came. Those reflexes worked like a piece of finely crafted machinery and were sharper than any blade.

After a subtle shift of his hand, Clint adjusted his aim and squeezed his trigger. He sent that bullet out with the precision of a master surgeon and put the chunk of lead exactly where he wanted it.

All of this took place in the blink of an eye. With two staccato blasts, everything was said and done. Smoke spewed from both men's barrels. Sparks filled the air as both bullets twisted their way into their targets. The round from Kyle's gun hissed about an inch away from Clint's rib cage. Clint's shot drilled a hole through Kyle's lower leg just above his ankle.

"Son of a bitch!" Kyle shouted as the pain ripped through him. As soon as those words were out of his mouth, he tried to take a step and wound up crumpling over as if he'd simply forgotten how to stand.

Kyle dropped over and landed not too far away from where Stewart was still writhing on the floor. So far, Stewart hadn't said much of anything because the pain he was feeling made it difficult for him to do more than suck in some air and push it out again.

Slowly, Clint got back into an upright position. He knelt at first, keeping the Colt aimed in front of him. Once he saw that he'd succeeded in knocking both men off their feet, he stood up all the way. He did not holster the Colt just yet, however.

Keeping the modified pistol at hip level, Clint walked over to Kyle and Stewart so he could reach down and take their guns from them. All in all, Clint couldn't be happier with his marksmanship. The other two weren't quite so pleased.

"You bastard!" Kyle squealed. "I can't walk no more!"

Clint looked at both men's wounds and saw that while each of them was in a world of hurt for the time being, they weren't permanently damaged. More importantly, neither of them were about to go anywhere.

"Would you rather be dead?" Clint asked.

It was Stewart who answered that question. Pulling in another breath, he looked up at Clint and said, "N . . . no."

"Then stop your griping."

FORTY-FOUR

Less than an hour later, Clint was riding out of town. Eclipse didn't have any extra bundles tied to his back this time. Instead, Clint held on to two other sets of reins belonging to Kyle's and Stewart's horses. Those two animals bore the weight of the three prisoners, all of which had several coils of rope to keep their bandages in place.

When Clint had been picking his targets inside that shop, he'd purposely gone after spots that would hurt like the dickens and take the other men off their feet. That way, apart from a steady flow of bitching and moaning, the ride back to Waylon City was relatively peaceful.

Jerry had resigned himself to his role as a captive, and the other two were in no condition to run away from anything moving faster than they could roll. None of the three were happy about their situation, but they kept their mouths shut, hung limply over their horses' backs, and tried not to fall off.

Clint rode straight into town, but was spotted about a mile outside of Waylon City's limits. Although they hadn't encountered a posse anywhere along the way, Clint and his three prisoners had a good-sized escort by the time they came to a stop. Marshal Packard along with a few unfamiliar faces surrounded Clint and held him at bay with rifles.

"You get sick of hiding out like a dog, Adams?" Packard asked.

Clint shrugged. "Sure. I just knew it would be a matter of time before you caught up with me."

The fact of the matter was that some of his statement was true. Although he knew there wasn't much to fear from Packard himself, Clint knew the mess would come back to haunt him unless he saw to it that it was cleaned up. To that end, he tossed all the reins he'd been holding and allowed Marshal Packard to personally take the Colt from its holster.

"I want a trial, Packard," Clint said now that he could see a good-sized crowd gathered around. "A real trial."

"You had your trial."

"I want a jury and my due process this time around."

"Why?" Packard sneered, nodding toward the trussed up men tossed over the spare horses. "You go and shoot yourself some witnesses to speak on your behalf?"

"No," came a voice from the crowd. "He's got witnesses and he needs to have a trial."

Packard swung around to look at who'd stepped forward and found himself staring into one of the most respected faces in town. "What're you talking about, Doc?"

Cohen held his head high and walked to stand between Clint and some of the guns pointed at him. "You heard me. I don't remember hearing about a trial. I sure as hell would have gone to see it."

"Why would you bother?"

"Because I saw those three men lurking about when Tony Ackerman was shot. Go ask Emma and she'll tell you herself that Clint Adams was trying to protect himself as well as her when he was forced to shoot Tony. I'm sure Mister Adams could explain himself just fine if he was given half a chance."

"Don't you listen to this man, Doc. He's a killer."

"Men carry guns to protect themselves. It's for a jury or a judge to decide what's what. Not just one man."

"You never had a problem with the way things were done." Shifting around to look at the entire crowd, Packard added, "None of you have."

"Then maybe that should change."

It wasn't Doc Cohen who'd made that suggestion. In fact, it was the middle-aged woman who'd spoken to Clint in the tailor shop who stepped forward to stand with Clint. "I saw those men there as well, but never said anything because I was afraid." As she looked at those three wrapped up like presents beneath a Christmas tree, the nervousness left her eyes.

A hush fell over the crowd as Marshal Packard looked over to the man Clint recognized as the judge who'd paid him that short visit so long ago. After a few moments, the judge shrugged and nodded to Packard.

"All right," the marshal said. "You can have your second trial, but until then you men are going to jail. All four of you."

Clint smirked and allowed himself to be pulled down from the saddle by some of Packard's new deputies. "Just as long as I can have my same bed," Clint replied.

There wasn't one more trial.

There were two.

With Tony Ackerman unable to bully anyone on his own behalf, character witnesses weren't hard to come by. Several of those witnesses reported seeing Ackerman baiting Clint into a fight. The real break came when the three men Clint had captured took their turns on the witness stand.

Stewart was the first to crack, and Jerry crumbled soon after. They admitted to being paid by Ackerman to find a good spot where they could hide so they could be the ones to shoot Clint in the back before Ackerman was hurt.

All three of them, it turned out, lost their nerve the moment they suspected that Clint had spotted them hiding in the shadows. That yellow streak running down all their backs saved the three would-be assassins when they were put in the hot seat for their own trial.

By the time the second trial was held, Clint was a free man as well as a star witness. In the end, the charges against Kyle, Jerry, and Stewart were reduced to reckless endangerment and acting as public nuisances.

"Guilty as charged," the judge said after slamming his gavel on the table in front of him.

Since no one had been hurt, Marshal Packard let the embarrassing matter of Clint's jailbreak drop.

Since the three prisoners turned out to be known associates of a man who was better off dead, no one had much to say about the wounds Clint had given to them.

Truth be told, everyone involved in the trials was just happy to see Clint leave. Watching the gallows being pulled down as he rode Eclipse out of Waylon City, Clint had to admit he was just as happy to oblige them.

J. R. ROBERTS

THE GUNSMITH

**Explore the exciting Old West with one
of the men who made it wild!**